W9-CEA-321

"You are so beautiful, March. So absolutely beautiful," he murmured throatily as his mouth began to descend toward hers.

She blinked, stiffening in his arms. "What—what are you doing?" she gasped.

He smiled self-derisively, his lips only inches from hers now. "Guess," he teased softly.

A speechless March was just too irresistible, and as Will slowly bent his head to claim the moist softness of her lips he knew he had no intention of even trying....

THE CALENDAR BRIDES

They've got a date—at the altar!

International bestselling author
Carole Mortimer has written more than
115 books, and now Harlequin Presents®
is proud to unveil her sensational new
CALENDAR BRIDES trilogy.

Meet the Calendar sisters:

January—is she too proud to become a wife?

March—can any man tame this free spirit?

· May—will she meet her match?

These women are beautiful, proud and
spirited—and now they have three rich,
powerful and incredibly sexy tycoons ready
to claim them as their brides!

Available January, March and May 2004

Carole Mortimer

THE UNWILLING MISTRESS

THE CALENDAR BRIDES

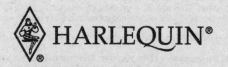

HARLEQUIN®

TORONTO • NEW YORK • LONDON
AMSTERDAM • PARIS • SYDNEY • HAMBURG
STOCKHOLM • ATHENS • TOKYO • MILAN • MADRID
PRAGUE • WARSAW • BUDAPEST • AUCKLAND

ISBN 0-373-12382-5

THE UNWILLING MISTRESS

First North American Publication 2004.

CHAPTER ONE

'GOOD morning,' a voice greeted cheerfully, quickly followed by a more tentative, 'er—again…?'

March closed the folder containing the figures she had been frowning over, not at all happy with what she saw there, taking several seconds to automatically assume the polite smile reserved for the clients entering the estate agency where she worked.

Although that polite smile turned back to a frown as she looked up and realized the reason for the man's second tentative query.

It certainly was 'again', wasn't it?

She sat back in her chair, her gaze rueful now as she looked up derisively at the man standing in front of her desk.

Under any other circumstances she would have found this man extremely good-looking.

Very tall, probably aged in his mid-thirties, with a tangible air of self-confidence, he had slightly overlong silver-blond hair, with hard, sculptured features, his eyes the colour of sky on a clear summer's day—which today certainly wasn't!

It was snowing outside—and not half an hour ago this man had neatly slipped into the car-parking space directly outside here that March had been about to parallel-park into!

The politeness of her role as Receptionist in this busy estate agency, and indignation that instead of being able to park outside she had had to park half a mile away and walk back through the snow, warred inside her.

The latter easily won!

'Correct me if I'm wrong,' she bit out caustically, 'but the last time we saw each other I believe you ensured that I would not have a good start to my morning!'

The man gave a pained wince. 'You remember me.'

March eyed him scathingly. She was hardly likely to forget him!

She had been absolutely furious earlier when she'd turned to begin her parallel park and seen this man neatly driving his red sports car into the space instead. If she hadn't already been late for work, due to the bad weather, she would probably have got out of the car and told him exactly what she thought of him. Instead she had driven around for ten minutes trying to find another parking spot, and then had to trudge all the way back in the falling snow. All the time cursing this man for his inconsideration!

The fact that the powerful red sports car had still been parked outside when she'd got back here had only added insult to injury.

Although the reason he had chosen to park in that particular spot was made obvious by the fact that he had now come into the agency. After wasting time by wandering to the newsagent's two doors down, if the newspaper under his arm was anything to go by. Well, it was his own fault if he had had to wait for her to open up for business; she wouldn't have arrived late at all if he hadn't stolen her parking space!

The man gave her a quizzical smile. 'We do seem to have got off to rather a bad start,' he acknowledged ruefully.

Yes, they had, but he was obviously a customer, and

she was the only one to have arrived in the office so far this morning.

March forced herself to once again smile politely. 'How may I help you, Mr...?'

'Davenport,' he supplied lightly. 'Will Davenport. Mind if I sit down—March?' he prompted after a glance at the name tag on the lapel of her suit jacket.

'That's what the chairs are for—Mr Davenport,' she pointed out dryly.

He lowered his long length into the chair opposite hers. 'Tell me, March,' he drawled, 'is everyone here as friendly as you?' A derisive smile curved his own lips now as he eyed her mockingly across the width of the desk.

March felt the colour warm her cheeks at this deliberate rebuke. Probably deserved, she allowed grudgingly. Although that didn't excuse his own high-handedness earlier.

'Only when they've had their parking space usurped!' she returned sharply.

He grinned unabashedly. 'I live in London.' He shrugged broad shoulders beneath the navy-blue sweater and thick overjacket he wore. 'Parking spaces there are up for grabs to the first taker!'

March felt slightly disarmed by that grin. He really was very good-looking, that overlong silver-blond hair falling endearingly over his forehead, laughter lurking in those deep blue eyes, the hardness of his features softened by the grin too.

But the fact that this man was breathtakingly handsome really wasn't the point, was it?

'I was the first taker!' she reminded impatiently.

He gave an irritated frown now. 'Perhaps we could move on?'

Yes, perhaps they had better. Clive, when he finally did put in an appearance, wouldn't be too happy with her for alienating a customer—perhaps their only customer on a day like today!

March drew in a deeply controlling breath, straightening some folders on her desk before forcing herself to resume that polite smile. 'Are you interested in buying a property in the area, Mr Davenport?'

'No.'

Her eyes widened, grey-green eyes surrounded by thick dark lashes, the same colour as her below-shoulder-length hair. If he wasn't interested in buying a property, then why—?

'I'm looking to rent a place for a couple of weeks,' he added mockingly.

Her brow cleared at this explanation. 'For the summer?' She stood up, moving to the filing cabinet behind her. 'We have some rather lovely cottages—'

'No, not for the summer. For now,' Will Davenport corrected even as she pulled open a drawer.

March turned back to him with raised brows before glancing frowningly at the snow still falling outside. It was January, for goodness' sake, none of the people they had on their books rented the cottages out in winter—mainly because very few of the properties actually had any heating in them, apart from an open fire.

'I'm in the area on business for a few weeks.' Will Davenport obviously took pity on her confusion. 'I'm booked into a hotel at the moment, but I hate their impersonality,' he added with a grimace.

March really wouldn't know whether hotels were impersonal or otherwise, never having stayed in one. Living on a farm, the middle one of three sisters, brought up alone by their father since March was four, there had been very little money to spare for things like holidays. And since their father died last year, that situation had only worsened.

She suddenly became aware of the completely male assessment of Will Davenport's gaze as he studied her, from the top of her ebony head to the soles of her heeled shoes.

At twenty-six, she was tall and slender, with long shapely legs, smartly dressed in a navy-blue suit matched with a lighter blue jumper, pale magnolia skin, her make-up light, her lip-gloss peach, only the pointed determination of her chin indicative of the stubbornness of her nature.

Although Will Davenport obviously liked what he saw, his smile warmly appreciative now as he gave a mocking acknowledgement of his head at her questioning look.

Well, really!

He had literally pushed—parked!—his way into her life—and now he was looking at her as if she were the tastiest thing on the menu!

March moved abruptly to resume her seat behind the desk, glaring across at him as she wondered how much longer Clive and Michelle were going to be; quite frankly, she had had enough of trying to deal with Will Davenport for one day.

Clive Carter and Michelle Jones were not only partners in the estate agency of Carter and Jones, but they also lived together on the outskirts of town. The fact that neither of them had arrived yet had to mean that the snow was delaying both of them. More was the pity!

As the receptionist, March usually only answered the telephone and passed clients on to either Clive or Michelle. Something she really wished she could do with this particular client!

'I'm afraid Mr Carter and Miss Jones aren't in the office at the moment,' she began crisply.

'I think I can see that for myself, March,' Will Davenport drawled mockingly.

March flushed irritably at his obvious sarcasm. 'What I'm trying to say is that I think it would be better if you called back later and spoke to one of them,' she snapped, grey-green eyes flashing a warning of her rising temper.

His mouth twisted. 'You aren't qualified to show me details of any properties for rent in the area?'

If he was meaning to be insulting—and he probably was!—then he was succeeding.

March frowned. 'Of course I can show you the properties, Mr Davenport—'

'Then perhaps you had better do so,' he suggested dryly.

March drew in a deeply controlling breath as she desperately tried to resist the urge she had to wipe that confidently mocking smile right off that sculptured mouth!

The man was infuriating! Not only that, he was arrogant, mocking, and he had the cheek to—

Wait a minute… He was looking for somewhere to rent. She might just have the perfect place for him, at that!

Will wasn't sure he altogether liked the cat-who-had-swallowed-the-cream smile now curving March's lips. As if she knew something he didn't…

Not that he could altogether blame her for being initially annoyed with him—he had taken her parking space earlier, something that had obviously infuriated her.

He had felt more than a little guilty about that when he'd entered the estate agent's a short time ago and recognized her as she sat behind the desk, but that guilt had since turned to admiration. March was absolutely beautiful when angry. Those unusual grey-green eyes sparkled with the emotion, her pale skin having a blushing hue, as for her mouth—!

But he wasn't quite so comfortable with that quietly satisfied look on her face now...

'Tell me, Mr Davenport...' she leant across the desk confidingly '...are you particularly looking for somewhere here in town, or would somewhere further out be of any interest to you?'

Will eyed her warily. 'That depends in which direction out it was,' he answered guardedly.

As far as he was concerned, the job he did was completely harmless, moreover he was completely professional, but he had learnt from experience that not everyone looked on it in the same way. The fewer people who knew the reason for his presence in the area, the better it would be. For the moment.

'Over towards the village of Paxton,' March told him lightly. 'If you don't know where that is—'

'I do,' he cut in lightly. 'Towards Paxton would be perfect.'

March looked startled. 'It would...?'

'Perfect,' he repeated mockingly.

She could have no idea how perfect. In fact, it was exactly where he wanted to be. Staying in the area would mean he wouldn't have to keep driving out there, could blend into the scenery more easily, and so not make himself quite so conspicuous to the locals. Certain locals in particular!

March looked a little less certain now. 'The property I have in mind is on a farm in the area, not a cottage but a studio-conversion over a garage.'

'Sounds good.' He nodded. 'When can I see it? I would really like to check out of the hotel and get moved in as quickly as possible,' he added briskly at her surprised look.

She blinked at his decisiveness. 'I'm not completely sure that the owners would be interested in a winter let, so I would have to call them first and check—'

'Go ahead,' he invited smoothly.

March looked totally nonplussed now. Obviously she wasn't used to things moving quite this quickly. Well, she would have to get used to it, because Will didn't have any time to waste, wanted to get the job done, and then get the hell out of Dodge City. Before anyone started baying for his blood!

'Time is money, March,' he prompted dryly.

She blinked, her expression suddenly becoming wistful. 'My father used to say that,' she explained huskily at his questioning look.

'Used to?' Will repeated softly.

March sat up straighter in her chair, that flush returning to her cheeks, as if she had said too much. 'He died,' she bit out abruptly, at the same time picking up the telephone. 'I'll call the farm now,' she told him curtly.

Will watched March rather than listened to her conversation. She really was beautiful. Perhaps his time in Yorkshire wasn't going to be quite as lonely as he had initially thought. If he could get past the prejudice she felt towards him because he had 'usurped her parking spot', that was!

'Will one-thirty suit you for viewing, Mr Davenport?' March looked enquiringly across the desk at him, her hand over the mouthpiece as she spoke. 'Even farmers stop for lunch,' she informed him dryly as he raised blond brows.

'Fine,' he snapped, knowing she was deliberately mocking him.

Was it so obvious that he had been born and lived in cities all his life? Probably. But he liked what he had seen of Yorkshire so far, and this part of the county was particularly beautiful.

Although he still had that niggling feeling that there was something not quite right about the property March was sending him to see. Perhaps the farmer had a particularly fierce bull he liked to set on strangers? Or perhaps a pack of hounds? Or perhaps she just found the idea amusing of placing Will, a man obviously used to the amenities of the city, on a farm?

It might be at that; as far as he was aware, he had never set foot on a farm in his life. But there was a first time for everything, and from the sound of it, the location was perfect...

'That's settled then, Mr Davenport,' March told him briskly as she ended the call, writing an address down on a piece of paper before handing it to him. 'I'm sure that either Mr Carter or Miss Jones would be only too pleased to accompany you—'

'No, thanks,' he cut in briskly. 'I would rather find my own way around.'

She nodded. 'But please feel free to call back and speak to either Mr Carter or Miss Jones if you find this particular rental unsuitable for your needs.'

Giving Will the clear impression that she already knew it wasn't going to be!

Which only incited him into wanting to take that satisfied little smile off her beautiful face! 'March, would you have dinner with me this evening?'

He almost laughed at the sudden stunned look on her face. Almost. Because even as he made the invitation he knew that he really did want her to have dinner with him…!

She was prickly and outspoken, absolutely nothing like a receptionist greeting the general public should be, but at the same time he liked her outspokenness, that sparkle in her eyes, and her beauty was indisputable.

She seemed to gather her scattered wits together with effort, straightening in her chair even as she began to shake her head. 'I don't think so, thank you, Mr Davenport,' she refused tautly, those dark lashed grey-green eyes sparkling with indignation now.

He quirked blond brows. 'No taking pity on a stranger in the area?'

Her mouth twisted derisively. '*Being* a stranger here, you may not have heard, Mr Davenport, but we had a stalker in the area until he was caught quite recently.'

As it happened, Will had heard—although he wasn't quite sure he liked her implication!

'As I recall, the man was a local,' he reminded dryly.

'Yes, he was,' she confirmed abruptly, her cheeks pale now. 'But that's all the more reason to be doubly wary of strangers.'

He gave an acknowledging inclination of his head. 'Maybe I'll come back tomorrow and ask again—I won't be a stranger then!'

March gave the ghost of a smile. 'You can try,' she challenged.

But he would be wasting his time, her words clearly implied. Pity. He would have liked to get to know her better.

'Thanks, anyway, March.' He stood up to leave. 'I'm expected at one-thirty, you said?'

'Lunchtime,' she confirmed dryly.

Good, that would give him time to complete the other

business he had in town. Although, so far, that was proving more difficult than he had imagined.

He turned back to March. 'I don't suppose—no,' he answered his own question, shaking his head ruefully. 'Sorry.' He grimaced at her enquiring look. 'I'm making enquiries about a friend of mine who was staying at the hotel until a few days ago, but as he was another stranger, I don't suppose you would know anything about him, either!'

March eyed him mockingly. 'I don't suppose I would.'

Will grinned. 'Never at a loss for words, are you?' he said admiringly.

'Only when invited out to dinner by a complete stranger,' she mocked her own momentary lack of composure a few minutes ago when he'd made the invitation.

He chuckled softly. 'It isn't too late to change your mind about that...?'

'I'll pass, thanks,' she returned smilingly, her attention distracted behind him at that moment as the bell rang over the door to announce a new arrival.

'Thanks for this, March.' Will held up the piece of paper with the address on it. 'You can have my parking space now, if you want it,' he added goadingly.

March gave him a look from beneath deliberately frowning brows. 'I believe that was *my* parking space, Mr Davenport—and I won't bother now, if you don't mind.' She laughed in spite of herself.

Will nodded politely to the man and woman who had just entered, deciding from their business suits, and general air of ownership, that they were probably the Mr Carter and Miss Jones that March kept referring to.

He glanced back inside before driving away, raising a hand in parting to March as he saw she was looking out of the window at him, too. Still with that self-satisfied smile curving her lips, the little minx.

Pity she had turned down his dinner invitation. Although, perhaps with the controversial circumstances of his being in the area, it was probably better not to involve her.

From what he had already been told, he was going to have enough trouble with certain members of the community, without becoming personally involved with another one of them.

As Max appeared to have done…

CHAPTER TWO

MARCH wasn't in the least surprised to see the powerful red sports car still parked in the yard when she arrived at the farm that afternoon shortly before two. In fact, she had counted on it!

Will Davenport, with his good looks and air of sophistication—his lack of apology for taking her parking spot!—had totally rubbed her up the wrong way this morning. Well, the boot was on the other foot now—as he was shortly going to realize.

Wednesday was half-day at the agency, a fact she had been very aware of when she'd made the appointment for Will Davenport to view this rented accommodation at one-thirty.

'You really didn't have to bother to come all the way out here, you know,' Will Davenport's unmistakable voice drawled from behind March as she turned to get her bag from the back of the car. 'I did tell you I would be able to manage for myself,' he added with confident dismissal.

March slowly straightened before turning to give him a mocking smile. 'And have you?' she taunted.

'Of course.' Will stepped aside so that the person standing behind him was now visible. 'Apart from signing on the dotted line, I believe May and I have settled everything.' He grinned his satisfaction.

March turned to the young woman who now stood beside Will. 'I don't think we have a dotted line for Will to sign on, do we, May?' she prompted lightly.

Her sister smiled. 'Not that I'm aware of, no,' she drawled, at the same time now giving March a quizzical look.

May, as the eldest of the three sisters, had always been the more level-headed one too; it didn't need two guesses to know that she was not going to be pleased with March for the little trick she had played on Will Davenport today.

Never mind; it had been worth it—just to see the puzzled expression as his gaze moved frowningly between the two sisters!

'"We"?' he finally prompted slowly, his expression wary now.

March gave a satisfied grin. 'I didn't come here to check up on you, Mr Davenport—I happen to live here!' she took great delight in telling him.

To say he looked stunned by this disclosure had to be an understatement; he looked as if someone had just punched him between the eyes!

Yes, he looked stunned—and something else, March realized as his expression instantly became guarded. She had thought, from the little she had seen of him, that once Will got over the surprise at learning that it was her family farm she had sent him to, he would laugh about the situation. But obviously she had misjudged his sense of humour, because he certainly didn't look as if he felt much like laughing.

'It was only a joke, Mr Davenport,' she told him ruefully. 'Not a very clever one at that,' she allowed dryly. 'After all, we do have the studio for rent, and you did say you were looking for somewhere in the area...' She trailed off as she could tell that, far from seeing the funny side of the situation, he was now frowning darkly.

'The two of you are sisters,' he realized woodenly.

'I don't think you get any Brownie points for guessing that!' March grinned as she moved to stand next to May, the likeness between the two women more than obvious, both tall and dark-haired, their features similar, only the eyes a different colour, May's a clear emerald-green.

Will Davenport didn't return her smile. In fact, he seemed momentarily at a loss for words.

'Why don't you come into the farmhouse and have a nice cup of tea, Mr Davenport?' May briskly took charge of the situation, shooting March another reproving look as she took hold of Will's arm to urge him towards the house.

March followed slowly behind them. Some people just didn't have a sense of humour, she decided scornfully. It had only been a joke, for goodness' sake. And he had seemed to like the studio well enough before he'd realized she lived here too.

Maybe that was his problem, she realized a little disgruntledly. Perhaps he thought she might try to follow up on his earlier dinner invitation? That she had done this for some hidden reason of her own?

Well, he needn't worry, she had no intention of bothering him even if he did move into the studio for a couple of weeks; she was out at work all day, and busy with chores about the farm the rest of the time. Besides, she had the distinct feeling that Will Davenport was way out of her league...

'Put the kettle on, March,' her sister instructed firmly once they were in the warmth of the kitchen, Will Davenport still not looking any happier as he sat at the kitchen table. 'You obviously had no idea that this was March's home, too?' May prompted as she sat down opposite him.

'None at all.' He seemed to rouse himself out of his

stupor for a few seconds as he looked up at March. 'You would be March Calendar?'

She grinned. 'I certainly would.'

May frowned across at March before turning her attention back to their visitor. 'My sister sometimes has a warped sense of humour—'

'Oh, for goodness' sake!' March cut in impatiently. 'It was only a little joke. What possible difference can it make that I live here too?' she added irritably.

May sighed. 'Well, if I were in Will's shoes—'

'Which you obviously aren't,' March taunted; Will Davenport's shoes, indeed all his clothes, looked much more expensive than anything they could afford!

Her sister glared at her. 'March, when are you going to learn that you just can't do things like this? You're twenty-six years old, for goodness' sake, not six!'

Her cheeks became flushed at her sister's rebuke. 'It was a joke,' she repeated incredulously.

'It may have been—'

'It really is all right, May,' Will Davenport cut in lightly. 'March was just settling a score from this morning. Right?' He looked at her with narrowed blue eyes.

March shrugged. 'Well, I thought it was funny,' she muttered disgustedly.

And, no matter what May might say, it was funny. But March also knew the reason for May's concern; the money they would receive from letting the studio for two weeks would come in very handy. Any extra money always came in handy on a small farm like this one!

Will Davenport seemed to visibly relax. 'It was. It is.' He nodded ruefully. 'You see, May, I rather inconvenienced March this morning by ''usurping'' her parking space,' he explained wryly, at the same time shooting March a derisive look. 'This was obviously pay-back time.' His gaze was mocking on March now. 'Well, I'm afraid the joke is on you, March—because I have every intention of renting the studio for a couple of weeks. If that's okay with you?' He turned back to May.

'Hey, I live here too,' March defended ruefully.

'I think we're now all well aware of that fact!' May bit out impatiently.

Will Davenport began to smile, the smile turning into a chuckle. 'I think I'm going to enjoy my stay here, after all,' he murmured appreciatively.

'How could you have doubted it?' March came back mockingly, more than a little relieved that he had decided to stay after all; May really would never have forgiven her if he had decided not to simply because of the joke she had played on him.

'Only too easily, I would have thought,' May snapped, but she was smiling too now.

'I was thinking of moving in later this afternoon, if that's okay?' their new paying guest prompted lightly.

'He hates staying in hotels,' March put in derisively.

'Of course it's okay for you to move in today,' May confirmed. 'The studio should be thoroughly warm by this evening,' she added apologetically.

Something it obviously wasn't yet. Despite March's prompt call earlier so that May could go over and switch on the heating for their visitor. The studio hadn't been used since last summer, and so there hadn't been any heating on over there, either.

'Although you might prefer to come over and have dinner with us just for this evening?' May continued frowningly.

Now that was just going too far in March's opinion. The man was supposed to be renting the studio, completely independent of them and the farm, not moving in with them!

Will Davenport sat back in his chair to shoot her a knowing smile—as if he were only too well aware of what she was thinking. Which he probably was; she never had been any good at hiding her feelings! And with this man, someone who wouldn't be around long enough to matter, she didn't see why she should bother…

'How about that, March?' he drawled mockingly. 'We can have dinner together, after all!'

Oh, goody—she didn't think!

'Will invited me out to dinner earlier,' she told May bluntly as her sister looked slightly puzzled by the conversation.

May looked speculative now as she glanced first at Will Davenport and then more closely at March. 'Really?' she finally murmured enigmatically.

'Really!' March confirmed with a certain amount of resentment; the last thing she wanted was for her eldest sister to start thinking there was actually anything between Will Davenport and herself—because there wasn't. 'I said no, of course,' she said flatly. 'One can never be too careful, can one?' she added pointedly.

May turned to Will Davenport. 'Our younger sister used to sing at a hotel in town and was recently—involved, in the arrest of a man who was attacking people in this area,' she explained with a grimace.

'I sincerely hope you're not implying that I—'

'No, of course not,' May laughingly dismissed Will Davenport's mocking query. 'It just wasn't very pleasant, for January, or anyone else, for that matter,' she added with a frown. 'In fact, her fiancé has taken her away for a short holiday to get over it.'

'January?' Will Davenport echoed ruefully. 'Your parents certainly liked the names of months for their children, didn't they?'

'Personally, I've always been rather relieved I wasn't born in September,' March put in dryly. 'I can imagine nothing worse than going through life being called Sept! I suppose August wouldn't have been too bad—' She broke off as May spluttered with laughter.

'That wouldn't have suited you at all!' May explained with a grin.

'No, March suits you perfectly,' Will Davenport assured her wryly.

March gave him a narrow-eyed look as she placed the mug of tea on the table in front of him.

He returned her gaze with a look that was just too innocent for her liking. 'I've always looked on the month of March as brisk and crisp, the month that blows all the cobwebs away,' he drawled mockingly.

'That's March to a T!' May confirmed with another laugh.

'Thanks very much!' she muttered disgruntledly.

'You're welcome.' Will gave a derisive inclination of his head before turning back to May. 'Dinner this evening sounds wonderful—if you're sure I'm not intruding?'

Of course he was intruding. But, as March knew only too well, beggars couldn't be choosers, and the money he would pay them in rent over the next two weeks— once they had paid the commission to Carter and Jones, of course—would be very useful. The roof needed fixing on the barn, for one thing, and there were any number of small jobs about the farm that needed doing.

No, all things considered, she didn't mind this man 'intruding' for two weeks.

*   *   *

Will couldn't get over the likeness between the two sisters. He probably should have realized the connection when May Calendar had introduced herself on his arrival, but at the time he had had something much more important to occupy his mind.

As it still occupied his mind!

'You said your sister January is away on holiday with her fiancé at the moment?' he prompted lightly.

'Max.' May nodded with an affectionate smile. 'It's been rather a whirlwind romance, but we like him, don't we, March?' She looked up at her sister for confirmation.

Giving Will a few seconds' reprieve to come to terms with this latest piece of information. Max had got himself *engaged* to one of the Calendar sisters? Well, that certainly explained a lot!

'We do now,' March said with satisfaction.

'Oh?' Will prompted interestedly.

But not too interestedly, he hoped; he might have walked into the lion's den by accident—designed by March Calendar herself, if she did but know it!—but he was staying through choice.

He liked these two women. But especially March, with her quirky sense of humour and her outspokenness. It was refreshing to meet someone who said exactly what she thought. Or, if she didn't exactly say it, looked what she thought.

But he was still stunned by the fact that Max had become so personally involved with this family that he was actually going to marry one of them. Max had been a loner for as long as Will could remember, had always scorned the very idea of love, let alone marriage. Although if January was anything like March and May, perhaps the attraction was understandable…

Yes, he liked these two women, but whether or not they were still going to like him at the end of two weeks was another matter...

'Just a little family problem,' May answered him dismissively.

'Anything I could help with?' Even as he asked the question Will knew he had gone too far, could see the puzzlement in May's expression, March's more openly hostile.

'Not unless you're acquainted with Jude Marshall,' March bit out hardly. 'Max is a lawyer, originally sent here on Jude Marshall's behalf to buy our farm,' she explained at Will's frowning look. 'Which we aren't interested in selling!' she added with a pointedly determined look in May's direction.

A look Will was all too aware of. Dissension in the ranks? It certainly looked like it. May's next words confirmed it.

'We're thinking about it, March,' she told her sister.

'You might be—but I'm certainly not,' March snapped, two spots of angry colour now in the paleness of her cheeks.

May sighed before turning back to Will. 'You'll have to excuse us, I'm afraid, Mr Davenport—'

'Will,' he put in smoothly.

May smiled in acknowledgement. 'I'm afraid that whether or not we should sell the farm is an ongoing problem at the moment.' She gave a rueful shake of her head.

'May thinks we should, and I don't agree with her,' March snapped unnecessarily.

'And what does January think?' Will was intrigued about the younger sister, in spite of himself. Although he had already guessed at the rift between March and May over the situation…

'She'll go along with whatever I decide,' March announced triumphantly.

'Whatever *you* decide?' he prompted mildly; there were three sisters, shouldn't they all decide?

'Yes, you see May is—'

'I think we've bored Mr—Will,' May corrected at Will's gently reproving look. 'We've bored him with our problems long enough for one day, March,' she stated firmly as she stood up. 'The only thing that Will needs to know is that we definitely won't be selling the farm during the two weeks he wants to stay here,' she added lightly.

'That's a relief.' He smiled, preparing to leave as he took May having stood up as his cue to leave. 'I should be back by about five o'clock, if that's okay?'

May nodded. 'The garage beneath the studio is for your use.'

'Yes.' March grinned now. 'One fall of snow and you could lose your little car underneath it!'

What March described as a 'little car' was in fact a Ferrari! It was Will's pride and joy, the culmination of years of hard work. But, he had to admit, March was probably right about the snow! Yorkshire was having a particularly hard winter this year, many people having been snowbound in their homes until the last few days.

He gave a rueful smile. 'I'll try to remember that.' He nodded.

'Dinner is at seven o'clock,' May told him briskly as she walked to the door with him.

'Stew and dumplings tonight, isn't it, May?' March put in with a deliberately mocking smile in Will's direction.

She obviously didn't see him as a man who normally ate such nourishingly basic fare, and in one way she was probably right; he lived alone, had a busy life, and things like home cooking were not a luxury he could afford. Although he didn't think March would understand what he meant by that...

'It sounds wonderful,' he told May warmly.

'Just like your old granny used to make?' March put in tauntingly.

'March!' May winced laughingly.

'Let's hope so,' Will answered March dryly. 'My grandmother is a first-class cook!' he added challengingly, rewarded with the satisfaction of seeing that superior smile wiped off March's beautiful face!

'So was ours, and she taught us all to cook,' May assured him smilingly, lightly touching the sleeve of his coat in apology for March's outspokenness.

Strange that it was their grandmother who had taught the three sisters to cook, and not their mother...?

'There you are, March; something we have in common!' He grinned across at her.

'It's probably the only thing,' she muttered in reply.

Causing Will's grin to widen appreciatively. This woman really did have an answer for everything!

'Any chance of a home-made apple pie to go with the stew and dumplings?' he prompted hopefully. 'My grandmother makes the most mouth-watering pastry too,' he added dryly.

'Would you like us to get out the best silver and white table linen too?' March came back impatiently.

He raised mocking blond brows. 'Not unless it's what you normally do, no.'

'Hardly,' she scorned.

'It was only a suggestion about the pie.' He shrugged,

laughter gleaming in his eyes at March's obvious disgust with the whole conversation. 'Obviously if you can't make mouth-watering pastry—'

'Oh, but she can,' May put in, laughter lurking in her own eyes now as she listened to the exchange with obvious enjoyment. 'The art of making good pastry is having cold hands, I'm told,' she added mischievously.

'"Cold hands warm heart"?' Will returned teasingly.

'Let's leave my heart out of it,' March put in disgustedly.

Hmm, perhaps they had better, Will agreed with an inward frown. It was one thing to have a little fun at March Calendar's expense—as she had done earlier with him!—quite another for him to actually become involved with any of the Calendar sisters.

From all accounts, with Max's recent—surprising!— engagement to January Calendar, his friend had already fallen into that particular trap; he didn't think Jude would appreciate having Will do it too!

CHAPTER THREE

'I CAN'T believe I'm actually doing this,' March muttered as she rolled out the pastry for the apple pie.

May chuckled behind her as she laid the kitchen table for their evening meal.

'Will Davenport had better eat this after I've gone to all this trouble!' March added disgruntledly.

'Why did you send him here if you don't like him?' May sounded puzzled. 'Although, personally, I have to say I found him extremely charming.'

March continued to make the pie. It wasn't that she didn't like Will Davenport—she did, too much if the truth were told—but there was just something about him... Maybe she was imagining it, but she just had a feeling there was something he wasn't telling them.

Which was pretty stupid, when she actually thought about it; considering they really knew very little about Will Davenport, not even the reason he was in the area on business, there was a lot they didn't know about him!

'I hope the studio is warmer now,' May added worriedly, glancing out the kitchen window across to the garage/studio.

Will had arrived back at the farm over an hour ago, the lights on above the garage to show his occupancy, although they had seen nothing of the man himself.

Although that was soon going to change, March realized after a brief glance at the clock; in just over half an hour, Will was going to arrive for dinner.

'Did he say anything to you about why he's in the

area?' March prompted her sister casually as she cleared away her mess.

'Just looking around,' May answered distractedly, obviously still worried about the heating in the studio.

'At what?' March turned to her sister frowningly.

May shrugged. 'He didn't say.'

'Why didn't you ask?' March sighed frustratedly. 'I would have done.'

'I know you would have done.' Her sister gave a frustrated shake of her head. 'You didn't answer my question about why you don't like him?' she reminded shrewdly.

'I don't have to like the man in order to rent the studio to him,' March snapped, totally avoiding meeting her sister's probing gaze.

'Mercenary.' May laughed softly.

Not at all. But if she was going to manage to keep the farm at all then the studio would have to be let as much as possible to help pay the way. Which meant she couldn't be too choosy about whom she let it to!

Until quite recently the three sisters had been unanimous in their determination to keep the farm. But all that had changed in the last few weeks. January had just become engaged to Max, and it was pretty obvious that they weren't going to wait too long before getting married. And May, whose hobby was acting in the local amateur dramatic society, had recently been spotted by a film director who was interested in casting her in the film he was to make in the summer. Which left only March...

Maybe it didn't make much sense, or maybe she was just being her normal stubborn self, but March didn't want to sell the farm to this elusive Jude Marshall just so that he could include it in the neighbouring estate, which he had recently purchased, to make into an extensive health and country club! From the little she had been able to find out, the farm was to become part of the golf club he intended building on the complex. A golf club, for goodness' sake—when her family had lived and worked on this farm for generations.

March turned from putting the pie in the oven, frowning slightly. 'Talking about money—'

'When aren't we?' May put in disgustedly.

March smiled in sympathy. 'For once I wasn't referring to our own lack of it.' She grimaced. 'There's something going on at the agency that just doesn't make sense to me. Well, it does. But—' She broke off as a brief knock sounded on the kitchen door, rapidly followed by Will Davenport's expected appearance. 'Never mind,' March told her sister dismissively. 'I'll talk to you about it some other time.'

'Am I too early?' Will hesitated in the doorway at March's glare.

'Of course not,' May was the one to answer him welcomingly—cutting off March's more blunt reply!—quickly pulling Will inside and shutting the door to keep out the cold.

Something March was grateful for, knowing herself overwhelmed by a sudden feeling of uncharacteristic shyness.

She hadn't really thought that Will Davenport would actually want to rent the studio, had been, as he'd said earlier, just paying him back a little for his ungentlemanly behaviour of this morning. But now that he had decided to rent the studio, after all, she realized just how attracted she was to him.

Which was pretty stupid of her, in the circumstances; Will was only going to be around for a couple of weeks, would then leave to return to heaven knew where. Could even be—that dinner invitation apart!—returning to his wife and children, for all she knew!

But just looking at him beneath lowered lashes was enough to make her heart skip a beat. He was so tall his head almost brushed the beamed ceiling, that silver-blond hair falling endearingly across his forehead, blue eyes gleaming with good humour, lithely attractive in a thick blue sweater and faded blue denims.

Who was Will Davenport? More to the point, what was he doing in the area? Until she at least had the answer to those questions, perhaps she had better err on the side of caution—

Better err on the side of caution! What was wrong with her? Didn't she have enough on her plate, trying to find ways in which she could keep the farm, without adding the complication of being attracted to Will Davenport?

'Is that an apple pie I smell cooking?' He sniffed the air appreciatively, blue eyes gleaming with laughter as he looked across at March challengingly.

Her mouth twisted derisively. 'Somehow I doubt it,' she drawled. 'There is no smell of cooking from an Aga,' she added as she took pity on his look of disappointment.

'Your sister does love her little joke, doesn't she?' He grimaced at May.

'More like a twisted sense of humour,' May murmured affectionately, taking his jacket and hanging it behind the door. 'I hope eating in the kitchen is okay with you,' she added frowningly.

'It happens to be the warmest room in the house,' March put in bluntly; they always ate in the kitchen, so why apologize for it?

'This is great,' Will enthused. 'Once I'm settled in you must let me return the compliment and give the two of you dinner.'

That was an interesting concept—considering the studio was really only a bathroom, and one other large room that had to serve as kitchen, dining-room and bedroom. Very cosy!

'At a restaurant,' Will told March dryly as he was obviously able to read her thoughts.

That was the problem with having a mirror-face—she was completely unable to hide her feelings. But with any luck Will hadn't been looking at her earlier when she'd inwardly acknowledged just how attractive he was. Although she wouldn't count on it!

'Have a glass of wine,' she bit out abruptly, at the same time placing the glass down on the table ready for him to sit down. Maybe if he sat down the kitchen would no longer feel so cramped.

'Thanks.' He moved with fluid grace as he lowered his long length onto one of the kitchen chairs. 'So which one of you is the artist?' he prompted interestedly.

March's hand trembled so much she almost dropped her own glass of wine, looking across at him with widely dilated eyes, the sudden silence in the kitchen seeming oppressive.

Uh oh, looked as if he had put his foot in it again, Will realized with an inward grimace.

Unfortunately, there were so many things he couldn't discuss with the two Calendar sisters that he had decided to opt for what he'd thought was a neutral subject—only to realize by the tense silence that followed his casual enquiry that he had unwittingly walked into what looked like a minefield.

'Or perhaps I'm mistaken in thinking it was ever an artist's studio,' he continued evenly, knowing he wasn't mistaken at all.

His look around the studio at lunchtime had only been cursory, enough to tell him that it would be more than comfortable enough for the couple of weeks he intended staying in the area. A more leisurely mooch around on his return this evening had shown him the huge windows along one wall to allow in the maximum amount of light, pulling down the ladder to go up into the attic, that brief glance enough for him to have seen a paint-daubed easel and the stack of paintings against one wall.

He hadn't actually intruded any further than that brief look—and from the look of consternation now on May's face, the openly accusing one on March's, he was glad that he hadn't!

'I was,' March snapped coldly, her beautiful eyes now the grey-green of a wintry storm-tossed sea.

'Was?' Will echoed softly—dangerously? March certainly didn't look as if she cared to discuss the subject any further!

'She still is,' May briskly broke the awkwardness of the moment.

'No-I-am-not,' March bit out forcefully.

Ouch. He really had put his foot in it this time, hadn't he? It wasn't a feeling he was familiar with. Well educated, known and respected in his own field, he was accustomed to talking comfortably and confidently on any subject that came along. But not, apparently, when it came to the Calendar sisters!

He took a sip of his wine, giving March the time she needed to get past whatever the problem was, at the same time aware of the effort it took her to release the sudden tension she had been under. But why? So she painted in her spare time—what was the big deal?

'More wine, Will?' May offered, holding up the bottle invitingly.

'Thanks,' he accepted gratefully.

'The apple pie, March,' May prompted quietly.

Will waited until the younger Calendar sister had turned to the Aga before looking up at May with raised brows. She gave a barely perceptible shake of her head, enough to confirm that the subject of those paintings in the attic was not one he should pursue.

Not that he had intended doing so, anyway; March was prickly enough already, without adding to the problem.

Although his own curiosity about those paintings had certainly been piqued. What was wrong with them? Were they so amateurish that March simply didn't choose to discuss them?

Would he be violating his role as a temporary lodger if he were to go back up into the attic and take a look at them?

Probably, he acknowledged with an inner grimace. But he knew he wanted to take a look at them, anyway.

'You rented the studio, Mr Davenport,' March snapped as she seemed to read some of his thoughts now. 'At no time were you told that rental included the right to snoop around in the attic above.'

'March!' May muttered in obvious embarrassment at her sister's rudeness.

'It's all right, May,' Will assured her smoothly before turning back to March. 'I wasn't aware of that, March, but now that I am...' He shrugged, reluctant to actually state that he wouldn't intrude on the attic again, his curiosity well and truly roused now.

'Let's eat, hmm.' May seemed more than a little flustered by this sudden awkwardness.

As well she might be. Will had thought March Calendar completely uncomplicated, her emotions totally readable—even that brief moment of complete awareness of him she had felt when he'd arrived earlier!—but now he saw there was much more to her than that. Intriguing...

Was this the way it had been for Max? Had he also arrived here and taken the Calendar sisters at face value: beautiful, friendly, uncomplicated—only to find that they were all so much more than that? January Calendar certainly must be to have captivated Max, to Will's knowledge a confirmed bachelor, into falling in love with her.

Although the fact that Max was now engaged to marry the younger Calendar sister seemed to imply he was more than happy with the arrangement!

Will's smile faded somewhat as he realized he still had to find a way of breaking that little piece of news to Jude...

Although his good humour was somewhat restored by the aroma, and then the taste, of the promised stew and dumplings.

'Just like Granny makes?' March teased after his first mouth-watering taste, obviously not a woman who continued to bear a grudge, this morning's debacle over the parking space excepted.

'Better,' he assured warmly. 'Although don't ever tell her I said that, will you?' He grimaced.

She gave him a derisive glance. 'Somehow, I very much doubt the opportunity will ever arise!'

No, of course it wouldn't. Will had no idea what had even prompted him to say that.

March laughed at his confused expression, her earlier tension well and truly forgotten as she looked at him mockingly. 'Don't look so worried, Will; personally, I've always thought that old adage "the way to a man's heart is through his stomach" was a load of rubbish! If a man's only interested in what you can cook him for his dinner then forget it!'

He couldn't help chuckling at her disgusted expression. 'Maybe he'll be able to cook for you instead?'

'Now that sounds promising!' March said dryly.

'Do you cook, Will?' May put in mischievously.

Not quite the innocent peacemaker he had assumed after all, Will acknowledged with a rueful smile in May's direction.

'Tell me,' he murmured consideringly, 'are all the men in the area blind, deaf, and stupid? I can't believe you weren't all married years ago,' he explained at May's questioning look, a glance at the left hand of both women having shown them to both be unadorned by rings, and January Calendar had only recently—very recently!—become engaged to Max.

March grimaced at the comment. 'Maybe we're the ones who aren't interested,' she challenged.

And maybe three Calendar sisters were two too many? Although Max didn't seem to have had too much trouble getting past that particular problem!

'Good point,' Will dismissed, realizing the conversation was becoming altogether too personal.

He had wondered earlier whether accepting this dinner invitation was a good idea, knowing it would be better for all of them if he maintained a certain distance from the Calendar sisters. But March's obvious reluctance for him to accept the invitation had been enough to prompt him into doing exactly that!

What else might he feel goaded into doing before his time came to leave…?

'So if January is the singer in the family—' that little fact had been confirmed for him at the hotel earlier, and he'd even been able to view one of the publicity photographs of January used by the hotel; January Calendar was as beautiful as her two sisters '—and March works in the estate agent's, that must mean that you're the full-time farmer?' he prompted May curiously.

Farming seemed a very strange choice of career for any of these beautiful women, but Will knew for a fact, from the Calendar sisters themselves, but also from Jude, that they absolutely refused to sell the farm. At least, March did…

'Not exactly,' May laughed dismissively. 'You see—'

'May is an actress,' March put in with a proud smile in her sister's direction. 'She's been offered a part in a film—'

'Not yet, I haven't.' May looked embarrassed. 'Besides, March, I told you I haven't made my mind up yet about even going for the screen test.' She frowned at her sister reprovingly.

Will had a feeling that was something May had probably done a lot of over the years where the outspoken March was concerned!

'An actress?' he prompted interestedly. January was a singer, March was probably—no matter what she might claim to the contrary!—a good artist, and now it seemed that May acted; he couldn't help wondering how three young women obviously brought up on a farm could be so artistically gifted in such different ways.

But if May were to disappear for some time in order to make a film, that probably explained the current rift between the sisters concerning the selling of the farm. It was a start, at least…

'It isn't official yet.' May looked extremely uncomfortable. 'I have to go for a screen test next month—'

'A mere technicality,' March dismissed airily. 'You're going to walk through it,' she added with certainty. 'My sister is an extremely good actress,' she told Will proudly.

Something March, with her see-through face, could never be!

From the derisive smile March now directed at him he wasn't doing too good a job of hiding his own thoughts at the moment, either!

'Sorry.' But even as he made the apology he couldn't hold back his amused chuckle.

'No, you're not,' March acknowledged disgustedly, standing up to clear away the empty plates.

Will stood up too, moving across the kitchen to where March stood filling up the sink with soapy water. 'If I offer to help with the washing-up will I be forgiven?' he prompted huskily.

'Knowing how much March hates washing up—I wouldn't be at all surprised!' May was the one to answer him dryly.

But Will barely heard her reply, his breath suddenly caught in his chest as he found himself held mesmerized by March's luminous grey-green gaze as she turned to look up at him.

Her skin was like alabaster, smooth and creamy white, her mouth wide and sensuous, her neck arched with the delicacy of a swan, the baggy green jumper and fitted black denims she wore doing nothing to hide the allure of her slender body. A body he had been completely aware of from the moment he'd entered the farmhouse half an hour ago...

Once again Will found himself wondering if this was the way it had been for Max. A sudden, driving desire, a numbing of every other sense and sensation except this intense, spine-tingling awareness—

No!

Will wrenched his gaze away from March's, physically stepping away from her too, turning his back on her to further break the spell of sensuality that had briefly held him in its grip.

Will, Max and Jude had been at school together, losing touch briefly as they all went off to university to pursue their chosen careers, but those same careers renewing their friendship ten or so years ago. Now, at thirty-seven, despite having enjoyed numerous relationships, none of them had ever married. Somehow, after all this time, Will had assumed that none of them ever would. But Max, the one Will would have sworn was the least likely of the three friends to succumb, had fallen in love with the youngest Calendar sister.

Will did not intend falling into the same trap where March Calendar was concerned!

He drew in a harsh breath. 'Could I take a rain check on the apple pie?' he bit out tautly, deliberately speaking to May rather than March. 'I've just realized I have an important telephone call to make.'

'So much for helping with the washing-up!' March muttered behind him disgustedly.

It was a little ungrateful of him, he knew, but he needed to get away from here, needed to get some fresh air. Needed to clear his head, and his senses, of March Calendar!

'Take the pie with you,' May offered warmly, moving to pick the pie up off the side and place it in his hands.

'Hey, I like apple pie, too!' March protested.

'Will is our guest, March.' May turned to her sister warningly before giving Will a bright smile. 'I often think I failed miserably where instilling manners into March was concerned!' She gave a sorrowful shake of her head.

Once again Will felt himself being drawn into the warmth that was the Calendar sisters, his good humour returning as he smiled at May. 'March does have a point when she actually made the pie,' he murmured with a derisive grin in her direction.

'Oh, take it,' March dismissed impatiently. 'You probably don't have to worry about the calories, anyway!' she added disgustedly.

Neither did she if the willowy sensuousness of her body was anything to go by—

Not again. Will shook his head self-disgustedly. Okay, so March was beautiful, was quirky and outspoken too, as well as having a curvaceously sensuous body, but was that any reason for him to respond to her with the gaucheness of a callow schoolboy?

No, but it was reason for him to get himself out of here before he did something he would later regret—like kiss that derisive smile right off her pouting lips!

'I'm afraid there's no telephone in the studio,' May pointed out worriedly. 'But you can use the one here if—'

'Why doesn't he just move in here completely? We can charge him bed and breakfast prices then!' March put in scathingly.

Will's lips twitched with repressed humour as he saw

the way May winced at her younger sister's bluntness. March really was irrepressible.

And, despite her obvious despair at March's lack of manners, May was obviously staunchly protective of both her sisters. Making Will wonder how on earth Max, with his reserved haughtiness, had ever got the two older Calendar sisters' approval to marry their younger sister!

'That won't be necessary,' Will answered smilingly. 'I have a mobile in the car.'

'Well, of course you do,' March snapped derisively. 'How silly of us not to have realized that.'

May gave a weary shake of her head, obviously deciding that the best thing to do for the moment was to just give up apologizing for March's lack of manners. 'Enjoy the pie, Will,' she murmured ruefully. 'And if there's anything else you need, more towels, things like that, you have only to ask.'

'We'll send one of the maids over with it immediately,' March muttered disparagingly.

Will could see by the sudden fire that lit May's gaze that she wasn't always the calm, sensible sister, that she could be cutting herself when she felt it necessary. And he had a feeling that she would feel it necessary, where March was concerned, the moment he had gone out the door!

Which was a pity; he really didn't want to be the reason for any dissent between the two sisters. Even if March deserved it!

'This pie looks delicious, March, thanks,' he told her warmly.

She frowned at him suspiciously, but as he calmly returned her gaze that frown eased from between her eyes. 'You're welcome,' she finally murmured lightly.

'Thanks for dinner, May, it was great.' Will lingered

in the doorway, having absolutely no idea why he was having such trouble getting out of the kitchen now that it was time to go—especially as it was his own decision to do so!

'Don't forget to return the compliment,' March was the one to remind him pointedly.

He hadn't forgotten his earlier suggestion, Will acknowledged a little dazedly as he made his way back across the yard to the studio—he was just no longer sure he could cope with taking one Calendar sister out to dinner, let alone two!

He felt slightly disorientated after being with them for less than an hour, slightly dazed, as if he had drunk too much wine in a smoke-filled room—how on earth was he going to feel after spending an evening with them?

One thing he did know, he would have to clear his head before making his telephone call to Jude. A Jude, Will knew with certainty, who was going to be far from happy at Max's obvious defection to the enemy camp...

CHAPTER FOUR

'It's only lunch I'm suggesting, March, not an afternoon in a hotel bedroom!' Clive looked down at her mockingly as he perched on the edge of her desk.

March knew exactly what the male half of her employers was inviting her to—she also knew he wouldn't have made the suggestion about the two of them having lunch together if Michelle weren't out for the day showing a client over several different properties. Besides, she also knew that if Clive thought he could get away with it he would have no hesitation in taking her to a hotel bedroom for the afternoon!

While March was normally blunt to the point of rudeness—as Will Davenport had discovered to his cost the previous evening!—Clive's attentions over the last six months, whenever Michelle had been out of the office, were something March hadn't liked to tell her sisters about. There was nothing anyone could do about it, and they needed the money she earned from this full-time job. Besides, she doubted she was the first employee to suffer this sort of harassment.

It wasn't even that Clive was unattractive, because he wasn't; the epitome of tall, dark and handsome, with an easy charm as an added bonus. He just also happened to have been living with Michelle, the other half of this estate agency, for the last ten years!

'I said no, Clive,' she answered him calmly enough, grey-green gaze glacial as she glared her annoyance at him. For all the good it did. She had been saying no for

the last six months, but it didn't stop Clive from repeating the offer whenever the chance arose. 'You know
very well we can't just shut up shop for a couple of
hours and disappear off to lunch,' she dismissed briskly.
'Besides, I—I already have a date for lunch,' she added
with relief, having looked out of the window at that moment and seen a familiar red sports car drive slowly into
the square.

Will Davenport's car, with him sitting confidently behind the wheel as he found a parking space directly behind March's more serviceable Metro. He gave her a
friendly wave as he got out of the car and saw her watching him out of the window.

'If you'll excuse me.' March stood up hurriedly, moving quickly to open the door and call out to Will before
he could lock his car and just walk away. 'I'll be out in
a minute, Will,' she called out to him lightly, willing
him to wait for her.

He turned, a puzzled frown on that handsome face.
'Sorry?' He looked totally nonplussed.

'I'm just getting my coat,' she told him firmly, aware
that Clive had come to stand beside her in the doorway
now, a knowing smile curving his lips as he took in the
car and the man driving it.

Will turned his cool blue gaze on Clive Carter, that
gaze narrowing as he obviously saw the other man's too
familiar stance next to March, his arm resting against the
door behind her. 'No hurry,' Will answered in measured
tones. 'I'll come inside and wait for you,' he added with
another speculative glance at Clive.

That wasn't quite what she had wanted, March realized flusteredly as she made a quick grab for her coat
and handbag; having these two men size each other up
in silent appraisal was more than a little unnerving.

Especially as she could now clearly see the speculation in Clive's mocking grey eyes.

'Nice car,' he murmured softly. 'A Ferrari, isn't it?'

A Ferrari? March did a mental double-take on Will herself now. Okay, so she had realized it was a sporty-looking car, but all she basically required from a car was that it start up in the morning when she needed to get to work. But Ferraris cost tens of thousands of pounds, didn't they? Maybe there was more to Will Davenport than she had realized!

'Let's go,' she said decisively, grabbing hold of Will's arm to almost pull him outside. 'Walk!' she instructed once on the pavement, lips barely moving. 'And try to look happy about the prospect of taking me out to lunch!' she added as he simply stood looking down at her with mocking blue eyes.

'Certainly,' Will gave a derisive inclination of his head. 'As for happy…' He gave March no time to respond to his original comment as he bent his head, his lips taking possession of hers.

Well, there was happy and then there was *happy*…!

At that precise moment March felt so light-headed she didn't know what she felt, Will's mouth making a thorough exploration of her own, his arms firm about the slenderness of her waist.

If he was trying to impress upon Clive the fact that he was the one taking her out to lunch, he was obviously succeeding. If he was trying to render the usually voluble March speechless then he was succeeding in doing that too!

The softness of her body curved into Will's as if it were the other half of the hard contours of his, that silver-blond hair as soft and silky to the touch as she had imagined it would be—

As she had imagined it would be—!

Since when had she imagined touching any part of Will Davenport, let alone entangling her fingers in the thick softness of his hair as his lips sipped and tasted the softness of hers?

March pulled away from him abruptly, her gaze not quite meeting his as she stepped completely away from him. What on earth—

'Too "happy"?' he murmured teasingly.

Her head snapped up defensively, eyes flashing with anger. 'Let's just go, shall we?' she bit out furiously as she took a firm hold of Will's arm, knowing from her peripheral vision that Clive was still watching them as he stood in the doorway of the agency.

'Certainly, madam.' Will gave a mocking inclination of his head. 'Exactly where is it we're going?' he bent down to ask March conspiratorially as she almost frog-marched him along the pavement towards the busier high street of town.

March didn't even bother to answer him until they had turned the corner—and were safely away from Clive's curious gaze. Then she came to an abrupt halt, looking up at Will with glittering grey-green eyes. 'We aren't going anywhere—now,' she assured him firmly. 'You were obviously on your way somewhere else when you arrived, and I—'

'Yes—you?' Will prompted softly, a frown between his eyes now.

She felt the heat in her cheeks. 'I am on my way somewhere else, too,' she told him waspishly, still off balance from the kiss they had just shared. It might have been for Clive's benefit, but that didn't mean she hadn't been affected by it.

Affected by it! Her legs still felt slightly wobbly, her

breathing was erratic, and her lips tingled from the touch of Will's.

Will glanced briefly back in the direction they had just come from. 'Was he bothering you?' he prompted shrewdly.

She forced a derisive smile to her lips. 'Of course not,' she dismissed lightly. 'And even if he was,' she added resentfully as Will raised a sceptical brow, 'I happen to need the job.'

His mouth thinned. 'At the price of sexual harassment?'

'Don't be ridiculous,' she snapped irritably. 'Clive just likes to believe that every woman within a fifty-mile radius thinks he's God's gift to women,' she scorned. 'It doesn't mean anything.'

Will didn't look convinced. 'It looked like something to me,' he rasped.

'Well, it wasn't,' March insisted impatiently. 'Now please don't let me keep you any longer from whatever it was you came here to do.' She placed the strap of her bag very firmly on her shoulder, turning away.

His hand moved, his fingers curling firmly about her upper arm. 'At the moment I intend taking you out to lunch,' he told her determinedly, eyes narrowed as he glanced up the high street for a suitable eating place. 'Where would you recommend?' he prompted tersely.

'The White Swan will serve you an excellent lunch—' she nodded in the direction of the hotel across the road '—but for myself, I intend taking my sandwiches—' she pointedly took a foil-wrapped package from her handbag '—and sitting in the park for half an hour while I eat them,' she told him ruefully.

He grimaced. 'In this weather?'

Granted it was still January, and it had snowed yesterday, but that snow had already melted, and the wind wasn't too icy.

'In any weather,' she answered him dryly. 'Beggars can't be choosers,' she added caustically as she could see Will remained unconvinced.

But what was the point of earning every penny she could working, only to waste some of it on buying lunch, when she could just as easily bring sandwiches from home?

'My treat,' Will told her evenly, his hand tightening on her arm, his gaze narrowed as he negotiated the traffic as they crossed the road to the hotel.

'Will—'

'You don't want to make a liar out of both of us, do you?' He looked steadily down at her as she came to a stubborn halt on the pavement outside the hotel.

March gave a rueful smile as she shook her head. 'We both know you hadn't really arranged to take me out to lunch—'

'I have now,' Will cut in determinedly, easily pulling her along with him as they entered the hotel restaurant from the outside door, the warmth inside inviting, a lot of the tables already occupied.

'Will, this is ridiculous,' March continued to protest as a waitress showed them to a table in the window. 'I only said that earlier about the two of us having lunch because I—because I—'

'Yes?' He raised blond brows speculatively as he waited for her to sit down.

She gave a heavy sigh. 'Okay, so Clive was being a nuisance. But that's still no reason for you to have me foisted on you for lunch,' she added impatiently.

'Sit,' Will instructed firmly as he pulled her chair back for her.

By this time March could see that they were attracting a certain amount of attention; several other diners watching them curiously even as they made a pretence of eating their meal.

March sat—but only as a means of diverting attention away from the obvious difference of opinion between Will and herself.

'Woof,' she muttered pointedly beneath her breath, shooting Will a disgruntled look beneath lowered lashes.

Will grinned as he sat down opposite her. 'Woof, woof,' he came back laughingly.

March found herself returning that boyish smile. 'I really do feel awful for having put you in this position.' She made one last attempt to give him the opportunity to extract himself from feeling pressured into having lunch with her.

Will laughed outright at this comment. 'Tell me, March, have you looked in a mirror lately?'

'Sorry?' She frowned her confusion at what seemed like a complete change of subject.

He shook his head impatiently. 'March Calendar, you are a beautiful and desirable woman—no man in his right mind would accept he had ever had your company "foisted" on him!'

She gave him a mocking glance. 'When did you last see a psychiatrist?'

He grinned. 'Oh, I'm completely sane, I do assure you,' he murmured dryly. 'At least, I'm sure I was before coming here,' he muttered frowningly.

'Sorry?' She eyed him curiously.

'Never mind,' Will dismissed impatiently. 'Let's look at the menu, hmm?' he suggested briskly, promptly putting his own menu up in front of his face.

In truth, March was really quite pleased at this unexpected treat, couldn't remember the last time she had eaten out in a restaurant. Although there was one thing the two of them had better get straight...

'The answer is no,' Will bit out implacably after ordering a bottle of red wine to accompany the steaks they had both ordered.

March's eyes widened. 'I wasn't aware that I had asked a question,' she snapped.

His mouth twisted humorously. 'You weren't going to ask a question—you were about to make a statement. Am I wrong?' He quirked mocking brows, knowing he wasn't by the irritated flush that rose in her cheeks.

She scowled. 'I hate my see-through face!'

Will found himself laughing once again; no one could ever claim that March Calendar wasn't entertaining! 'Then you're in the minority,' he assured her softly.

She shook her head self-disgustedly. 'When I was little, my father always knew when I had done something wrong just from looking at me!'

She would have been adorable as a child, all the Calendar sisters would, Will acknowledged ruefully. But again he noticed that March hadn't mentioned her mother...

'Have the three of you been on your own for very long?' he prompted casually, surprised himself at how interested he was in the answer. At how interested he was becoming in anything that involved March Calendar!

She shrugged. 'Our father died last year. And we were all only babies when our mother—oh, no, you don't,' she rebuked decisively. 'No diverting me from what I was about to say earlier,' she told him firmly. 'If we're to have lunch together, and it appears that we are,' she accepted ruefully, 'then I insist on paying my share of the bill—'

'And I already said no,' Will reminded her calmly, a little disappointed that they had gone off the subject of her childhood and family, but accepting that he couldn't have everything his own way. Especially where March was concerned!

Although he had very much enjoyed kissing her earlier. In fact, he couldn't ever remember enjoying kissing any other woman as much. She had felt so right in his arms, and as for the effect holding and kissing her had had on his senses...!

Although that kiss was probably a subject he shouldn't refer to, either. March might have had little choice but to acquiesce earlier, but no doubt there were a few things she would like to say on the subject if given the chance!

He leant over the table, talking softly. 'March, men who drive Ferraris do not go Dutch with a woman on lunch. Okay?' he said pointedly.

It had come home to him very forcefully the previous evening that the Calendar sisters, while not exactly impoverished, certainly didn't have too much money to throw around; he doubted March, at least, would have agreed to rent the studio to him, or indeed anyone else, for a couple of weeks if she didn't have to. There was no way that he, with his own accumulated wealth, could possibly agree to March paying for half the lunch he had insisted she share with him.

'It really is a Ferrari?' she surprised him by saying.

He smiled. 'It really is.'

'Wow,' she breathed admiringly.

His brows rose. 'You like sports cars?'

'I like Clive believing I'm having lunch with a man who owns one!' Her eyes glowed mischievously.

Will couldn't help chuckling at her obvious glee at feeling she had put one over on her lecherous boss. Although his smile faded somewhat as he remembered the way the other man had stood so close to March earlier, almost as if he were stating some sort of proprietary claim on her...

'March—'

'Just leave it, hmm, Will,' she said firmly, sitting back as the waiter arrived to pour their wine. 'I'm more than capable of dealing with Clive,' she assured him dismissively once they were alone again.

Will didn't like the thought of her having to deal with the other man, had an intense dislike for predatory males who took advantage of the women who worked for them. One predatory male in particular!

'What is it?' he prompted as he saw March was frowning now.

Her smile, when it came, seemed slightly forced. 'Nothing,' she dismissed lightly.

He didn't believe her. 'It doesn't look like nothing to me,' he insisted firmly.

She seemed about to argue the point once again, and then gave a heavy sigh instead. 'You're in business, aren't you?' she prompted slowly.

Will felt himself stiffen defensively. 'I am,' he confirmed warily.

'Hmm.' March seemed not to notice his reticence, her thoughts inwards as she ran a finger around the rim of her wineglass. 'Well, is it illegal to buy something, for less than its value, in order that you can sell that—product on a few weeks later, at a hefty profit?'

'I would say that probably depends on what that—

product, is,' he answered slowly. 'And if you deliberately set out to defraud the original seller by knowing the product was undervalued.'

'That's what I thought.' She sighed heavily, obviously not particularly liking his answer.

'I wouldn't try it if I were you, March—your face would give you away!' he added teasingly.

She looked across at him blankly for several moments, and then her brow cleared, her expression indignant now. 'I wasn't talking about me!' she protested impatiently.

'Somehow I didn't think so.' He chuckled.

'Hmm. Well—' she frowned her irritation '—talking of business—'

'Ah, our lunch,' Will murmured with satisfaction as he sat back to allow the waitress to put the plates down on the table.

His relief at the interruption was due to two things. One, he was hungry. Two, he had no intention of pursuing the subject of his own business with March Calendar, of all people. He might end up with this delicious-looking lunch tipped over his head if he did that!

Although, as they began to eat their meal, he couldn't help feeling intrigued by her previous conversation. Who did March know who was defrauding people out of their money? Because he was pretty certain that she did know someone who was...

CHAPTER FIVE

'YOU had lunch with who?' May prompted speculatively as the two women sat and enjoyed a cup of tea together on March's return home from work that evening.

'You heard,' March muttered into her teacup, having decided it would be better for her to tell her sister about her lunch with Will today rather than have him perhaps drop it casually into the conversation at a later date. 'Very nice it was too,' she added lightly. 'I had almost forgotten what a nice steak tastes like.'

Obviously they never went short of food living and working on the farm, but such luxuries as fillet steak weren't usually on their menu.

Although one thing March had decided not to tell May; she had no intention of confiding in her sister about the kiss she had shared with Will.

She was still slightly shaken by her own response to that kiss. After all, what did any of them know about Will Davenport? Apart from the fact that he was good-looking, charming, and was obviously wealthy enough to drive an expensive sports car!

March still had no idea whether he was married or not. Although somehow she doubted it; he had certainly frowned on Clive's behaviour of trying to take advantage of his position as her employer.

But, despite several attempts on her part to introduce the subject during their lunch today, March had found out nothing further about Will's private life. Or, indeed, what exactly he was doing in the area.

'Well, that was nice of him.' May nodded. 'Uncle Sid said he saw Will's car over near Hanworth Estate this afternoon,' she added thoughtfully. 'I wonder what he was doing there?'

March was about to explain that Will had initially said this was the area he needed to be in, when a sudden thought occurred to her, her eyes widening in horror as the thought took root.

That horror only increased as she saw the same thought had occurred to May, her sister's face suddenly pale, her expression stricken. 'You don't suppose—'

'Do you think—?' Both sisters had begun to talk at once, both breaking off at the same time too, March's thoughts racing as she went back over the conversations she had had with Will since his arrival yesterday.

Yesterday? Was it really only a little over twenty-four hours since Will had entered their lives? It seemed like much longer!

It also seemed to March, as she remembered their conversations with him, that Will had found out a lot more about all of the Calendar sisters during that short time than they had about him…!

March's eyes narrowed as her original thought expanded and grew, to the point where she stood up restlessly to move to the kitchen window, glaring across the yard to where she could see the lights on above the garage to announce Will's presence in the studio.

'He's another one of them,' she bit out with sudden certainty, her hands clenching at her sides. 'Another one of Jude Marshall's henchmen! A wolf in sheep's clothing. Nothing but a snake in the grass!' She was building herself up to a rage now. 'Why, I've a good mind to—'

'We don't know that, March,' May soothed as she also stood up to look out of the window, green gaze narrowed speculatively across the yard. 'Although...' she added slowly.

'Exactly—although!' March snapped furiously. 'Another lawyer, do you think? Or something else?' Somehow she couldn't see Will as a lawyer. Max, yes, with his reserved aloofness, but Will was more outgoing than her younger sister's fiancé.

Max...

He would be sure to know if Will worked for Jude Marshall too; after all, until just recently, he had worked for the man himself.

It had been Max's efforts to buy their farm on Jude Marshall's behalf that had brought him into their lives in the first place. It had been falling in love with their younger sister, January, that had decided him that he was no longer suited to that sort of work.

But Max was in the Caribbean with January for two weeks, and March very much doubted that either of them were going to think of telephoning home during that time!

But if Will wasn't another of Jude Marshall's lawyers, what position did he hold in that corporation? Because March was pretty sure now that he was something!

'Something else,' May confirmed. 'Although we can't really be sure about that.' She hesitated.

'We can if we ask him,' March stated, moving with determined strides towards the kitchen door.

'No, I don't think we should do that,' May said slowly, halting March as she reached for the door-handle. 'Let's wait a while, hmm.' She frowned. 'See what else develops.'

'Like what?' March turned to challenge. 'We've already had Max creeping about trying to buy the farm out from under our noses. It isn't funny, May,' she reproved as her sister began to chuckle.

'Sorry.' May made an attempt to curtail her humour. 'I was just trying to picture our future brother-in-law "creeping" about anywhere!'

'Hmm.' March gave a rueful smile too at the image her sister created. 'I would love to see Jude Marshall's face when Max gets back from this holiday and tells him what he can do with his job!' she added with glee.

May shook her head. 'The two men are friends, March; I don't think Max will be as blunt as that. But you're right about seeing Jude Marshall's face.' She frowned. 'Personally, I would like nothing more than to meet the man face to face!'

'But, in the meantime, what do we do about our snake-in-the-grass lodger?' March reminded pointedly.

'Well, until we're sure—March, where are you going?' Her sister frowned as March picked up a cup and moved to the door.

She paused. 'To borrow a cup of sugar. Isn't that the usual excuse women use when they want to meet a man?' She raised innocent brows.

'You've been watching too many romantic films,' May admonished dryly. 'Besides, we've already met him,' she reminded.

March had done more than meet the man—she had kissed him, and been kissed by him. And if he really was what they suspected, he was going to regret taking advantage of that particular situation himself!

'So I meet him again.' She shrugged dismissively. 'I won't be long,' she added lightly before letting herself out of the house and moving swiftly through the cold of early evening to ascend the steps up the side of the garage and knock on the studio door.

Will did work for the Marshall Corporation, March was sure of it. And if that were the case, then he had known exactly who the Calendar sisters were before coming into the estate agency yesterday. In fact, she wouldn't put it past him to have engineered the whole thing!

The fact that she had been the one to send him here was irrelevant; if Will hadn't originally intended actually renting a property on their land, he had definitely jumped at the chance when it had been offered to him.

Yes, March now had no doubts that Will worked for Jude Marshall. Or that she was personally going to make him regret the day he had ever tried to deceive them!

Will was going over some figures as he sat at the table when the knock sounded on the door. He deftly rolled the papers up and put them away in a cupboard before answering that knock, knowing his visitor had to be one of the Calendar sisters; after all, apart from Jude, they were the only ones who knew he was here.

He burst out laughing as the light shining out of the open doorway revealed it was March standing on the top step, an empty cup in her hand. 'You look like Oliver, about to ask for some more,' he explained as she glared up at him.

She gave him a scathing glance. 'I've come to ask if we can borrow some sugar,' she told him waspishly. 'We've run out.'

'Certainly.' He smiled, holding the door open wider so that she could come inside. 'You're in luck; I've been food shopping today,' he told her as he rifled through one of the cupboards in search of the required sugar.

'Really? What else have you done today?'

Will gave her a brief glance over his shoulder. There

was a certain brittleness to March's voice that wasn't normally there; caustic, cutting, derisive, yes, but never brittle before. He wondered at the reason for it.

She returned his gaze steadily, one dark brow raised in challenge.

She had changed out of her business suit since returning from work, and now wore hip- and leg-hugging blue denims, with a deep green fitted sweater that brought out the same colour in those beautiful grey-green eyes.

Will felt a tightness across his chest as he looked at her, caught in that same lightning desire that had tautened other parts of his body earlier today when he'd kissed her.

He turned away abruptly. 'Here we are.' He brought down the sugar, the lightness in his voice sounding forced even to his own ears.

'Thanks,' March accepted as he poured some into the cup.

Looking more like the vulnerable Oliver than ever, Will acknowledged self-disgustedly, knowing that no one needed—or wanted!—his protection less than the feisty March Calendar.

'Was that all?' he prompted pointedly as she made no effort to leave.

'Am I keeping you from something?' March enquired lightly—at the same time making herself comfortable on one of the two chairs set either side of the small pine table provided for eating on.

'Not at all,' Will answered slowly, still eyeing her warily.

There was definitely something different about her this evening. Normally she had such a readable face, leading him to the correct assumption that she usually called a spade a spade, and to hell with everything else.

Usually... Because, unless Will was mistaken, she was hiding something tonight with that too-innocent expression.

'Thanks again for lunch, by the way,' she told him in that tightly clipped voice. 'I hope I didn't keep you from anything this afternoon?'

He leant back against one of the two kitchen units, his own gaze guarded now. 'Nothing of any importance,' he assured her dismissively. 'And it's I who should be thanking you for your company over lunch; there's nothing worse than sitting in a restaurant eating on your own.' Something he had done a lot of over the last ten years or so.

She gave a rueful grimace. 'So there was a method in your madness, after all,' she scorned. 'I should have known!'

'Why should you?' he returned easily, still uncertain of her mood.

Which was a little unsettling in March's case; it was unusual to meet anyone who showed their feelings—and spoke them—as clearly she did!

She gave a shrug. 'I knew it couldn't have just been gallantry on your part.'

He raised blond brows. 'You don't believe I can be gallant?'

March gave a derisive smile. 'There are very few men around nowadays that are!'

Will gave her a considering look. She seemed to be angry about something, that much he could tell. But whether or not that anger was directed at him—for whatever reason!—he wasn't sure yet...

'Would you like a cup of coffee, or possibly a glass of wine, now you're here?' he offered lightly, guessing by the way she had sat down so determinedly that she wasn't about to leave just yet.

'No, thanks, I've just had a cup of tea,' she refused stiltedly.

Almost as if drinking his coffee or wine might choke her. Will wasn't sure what was going on, but something certainly was.

He moved to sit in the chair opposite hers. 'What sort of man was your father?' he prompted curiously.

To say she looked startled was an understatement, her eyes widening before narrowing suspiciously. 'What does that have to do with anything?' she said guardedly.

Will shrugged. 'I merely wondered if your father had been one of the gallant men you referred to a few minutes ago.'

'Oh.' She blinked, seeming to straighten defensively. 'In that case—he was a blunt-talking Yorkshireman,' she said with obvious affection.

Will nodded. 'There's no doubting who you take after, then,' he returned teasingly.

There was no doubting her defensive attitude now, either, two bright spots of angry colour burning in the otherwise pale magnolia of her cheeks. 'Is there something wrong with being honest?' she challenged hardly, sitting slightly forward over the table. 'Personally, I abhor any kind of dishonesty.'

Will looked at her consideringly. Her eyes were sparkling with anger, her cheeks flushed, her whole attitude since she had arrived here a combatant one.

'March, what's wrong?' he prompted softly.

'Wrong?' she repeated stiffly. 'Who said there was anything wrong?'

'I did.' He sighed, not at all happy with the way this conversation was going.

One thing he had discovered during his conversations with March over lunch earlier today: he liked and admired her. He liked her blunt, no-nonsense manner, her complete loyalty to those she loved, namely her two sisters, and as for the way she looked... Everything about her was beautiful, her face, her hair, the willowy slenderness of her body, the habit she had of using her hands to illustrate a point as she was talking.

Something she hadn't been doing this evening...

Something was definitely wrong, and the sooner Will knew what it was, the better he would like it.

'March, has something—happened, since we had lunch together today?' he pushed determinedly. 'There's nothing wrong with May, is there?' he continued frowningly. 'Or your younger sister—January, isn't it?' he added with a casualness he was far from feeling.

If January and Max had telephoned from wherever they happened to be on holiday, and either March or May had happened to mention to Max the name of their temporary lodger—!

Will knew he couldn't indefinitely keep his reason for being here from March and May, but the longer he left telling them, the harder it was becoming to do so.

When he'd initially come to look at the studio with a view to renting, he genuinely hadn't known it was the Calendar sisters' farm that March had sent him to. Why should he have known? There were dozens of farms in the area, it just hadn't occurred to him that this could be the one where the Calendar sisters lived. Once he had become aware he obviously could have beaten a hasty retreat, but by that time March had arrived home, and the temptation to neatly turn her trick back on her by renting the studio had been too much of a temptation for him to resist.

At the moment both sisters seemed to like him, but learning of his connection to Jude Marshall, a man they both obviously disliked intensely, was going to change all that. And he already knew that having March hate him wasn't something he relished happening. Far from it!

Because he wanted March Calendar. Holding her in his arms earlier today, kissing the soft sensuality of her mouth, feeling the curves of her body moulding into his, had told him that he wanted her very badly. And, in the circumstances of his being here at all, she was probably a woman he could never have...

But, for this evening at least, she didn't know who he was or why he was here!

He stood up abruptly, moving round the table to take March's hand and pull her unresistingly to her feet. Only because she was too surprised to resist, he was sure, but for the moment that didn't matter.

'You are so beautiful, March,' he told her huskily. 'So absolutely beautiful,' he murmured throatily as his mouth began to lower towards hers.

She blinked, stiffening in his arms. 'What—what are you doing?' she gasped.

He smiled self-derisively, his lips only inches away from hers now. 'Guess,' he teased softly.

'But—but—'

A speechless March was just too irresistible, and as Will slowly bent his head to claim the moist softness of her lips he knew he had no intention of even trying...

CHAPTER SIX

MARCH was so stunned at the suddenness of finding herself in Will's arms that she didn't even try to resist, not when he held her, nor when his lips claimed hers.

And then it was too late to resist anyway. She groaned low in her throat as heated pleasure moved swiftly through her body, her mouth moving instinctively against his as he ran his tongue lightly across her lips, his hands moving caressingly down the length of her spine as he moulded her body against his.

A body that seemed to have turned to liquid fire, totally beyond anything March had ever known or felt before. Making her realize she wanted this man as badly as the arousal of his body seemed to say he wanted her!

His lips were moving heatedly down the length of her arched throat now, her skin seeming on fire where he touched, her own hands entangled in the silky hair at his nape as she clung to him.

Drowning. It must be like drowning, March decided dreamily, knowing there was no point in fighting against the tide of desire that enveloped her, any more than there would be fighting against a whirlpool that had her in its grasp.

Will felt so good against her fingertips, the buttons to his shirt proving no problem as she bared his chest to her searching hands, his skin warm and yet hard to the touch, hearing his own gasp of pleasure as her lips moved moistly against that heated flesh.

March groaned low in her throat as Will's hand cupped

her breast beneath the warmth of her jumper, feeling the nipple harden beneath his touch, the pleasure that coursed through her now making her legs feel weak, at the same time that every nerve-ending in her body responded to that caress.

His lips claimed her parted ones, his thumb moving rhythmically against her pouting breast now, his tongue seeking an answer to his unspoken message.

March answered that call, her response tentative at first, and then becoming more confident as she was the one to deepen the kiss. She couldn't stop this now. She just couldn't!

'Oops!' he gasped softly, his legs having caught the side of the bed, losing his balance slightly to sit down on the edge of the bed looking up at March with cobalt-blue eyes. 'March…?' he groaned uncertainly, his hands lightly clasping her hips.

She moved instinctively towards him, her hands cradling the back of his head as he pushed her jumper aside to kiss her bared breasts.

March really thought she was going to drown now, couldn't believe the heated emotions that swept over her as Will's lips and tongue paid homage to her uptilted breasts.

Where had this man been all her life? Why had it taken so long to find him? How had she existed for twenty-six years without—?

She hadn't been the one to find him—Will had been the one to deliberately find the Calendar sisters! As for where he had been all her life—!

'No!' she gasped, pushing him away from her, hastily straightening her clothing to look down at him with accusing eyes. 'What do you think you're doing?' she rasped accusingly.

Will blinked at the suddenness of her rejection, his eyes still dark with arousal, his cheeks flushed with desire. 'We were *both* doing, March,' he corrected slowly. 'And surely the "what" must be obvious,' he added ruefully, at the same time running a hand through the blond thickness of his hair.

The same hand that had touched and caressed her seconds ago! The same hair her own hands had been entangled in seconds ago!

She turned away, her movements jerky and uncoordinated, putting a hand up to her eyes as if to block out what had just happened between them.

But it would take more than that to shut out the memory of the intimacies they had just shared. If she ever could!

'March?'

She swallowed hard, straightening her shoulders defensively before turning to face Will. And just as quickly wished she hadn't; his gaze was still sleepy with desire as he looked at her quizzically, that aroused flush on his cheeks.

March shook her head, denying her own response to that arousal. 'I was referring to your own motivation for—for just now,' she finished hardly.

'Motivation?' he repeated softly, frowning slightly now. 'You're beautiful, March.' He smiled ruefully. 'Beautiful. Desirable. How could I resist you?' He shrugged self-derisively.

Her mouth tightened as she fought her own response to this verbal seduction. 'The fact that I'm also one of the Calendar sisters had nothing to do with it, I suppose?' she scorned harshly.

Oh, she knew she had agreed with May not to challenge Will on this point just yet, could even understand her sister's reticence in wanting to know more about the situation before confronting Will with it; but at the moment, who she was, what she was, was her only defence against what had just happened between them!

She watched as Will's cheeks lost that emotional flush, his gaze seeming wary now as it remained on her even as he slowly reached up to rebutton his shirt before standing up. The same shirt she had so ably unbuttoned only seconds ago!

March had no idea where any of those instincts had come from, had only known a need to be closer to Will than she'd already been, to touch his flesh in the way that he'd been touching hers.

But her response had been instinctive—could Will claim the same?

Will shrugged slightly, grimacing ruefully as he spoke. 'How much do you know?'

Not a lot, if the truth were known. In fact, only a growing certainty that Will worked for Jude Marshall in some capacity, if she were honest. But she didn't intend letting Will know that!

'I'm merely wondering what sort of man Jude Marshall is that he managed to buy the loyalty of both you and Max,' she replied insultingly.

The flush on the hardness of Will's cheeks was due to anger now. 'Jude hasn't bought me—or my loyalty,' he snapped tautly. 'Max's either, for that matter,' he added scathingly. 'You've met Max, he's going to marry your sister, for goodness' sake; does he seem like the sort of man who could be bought? By anybody!'

March met his angry gaze unflinchingly. 'And you?' she challenged scornfully.

His mouth tightened. 'I'm not employed by Jude, March,' he told her hardly. 'I am an architect, however.

A damned good one, if I do say so myself. But I choose who I work for.'

An architect. Which must mean that Will was here in order to draw up the plans for the health and country club Jude Marshall intended building on the Hanworth Estate. On land that the Calendar farm was smack in the middle of!

'You're William Davenport!' she said astoundedly, looking at him with new eyes now. 'You're the man that designed the award-winning building for the new museum in Leeds,' she realized dazedly.

He gave an inclination of his head. 'I am.'

March had visited the museum several times on trips to Leeds, the building a marvel of Victorian-style architecture, totally in keeping with its surroundings and ideally suited for its purpose.

No wonder this man drove around in a Ferrari; he was reputed to be in demand all over the world. Although at the moment he seemed to have settled for a very small part of it. Her part of it!

'And at the moment you choose to work for Jude Marshall,' she came back derisively. 'That only makes it worse!' she assured him disgustedly.

Will's gaze narrowed shrewdly as he gave her a searching glance. 'But until this moment you didn't know that, did you?' he realized slowly. 'Why, you little—' He broke off, giving a shake of his head. 'Minx!' he finished heavily.

March was too angry to feel anything else at the moment, but she knew that later, when she was alone, she was going to feel so much more than that. Which was why she intended clinging to that anger for as long as possible!

'In the circumstances, I think it will be better if you leave,' she told him coldly.

He arched blond brows. 'Now?'

'In the morning will do.' As long as he was gone before she came home from work tomorrow evening!

If she didn't have to see him, to know every day for the next two weeks that he was staying just across the yard in the studio over the garage, maybe she could at least put this evening to the back of her mind!

'No.'

March gave him a sharp look, her eyes widening indignantly as he returned her gaze unblinkingly. 'What do you mean "no"?' she rasped disbelievingly.

Will shrugged. 'I acknowledge there's no written contract, but there is a verbal agreement between your sister and I. I've already paid over two weeks' rent in advance—'

'We'll return the money to you!' March cut in heatedly. Although quite how they were going to do that, she wasn't completely sure; May had informed her earlier that she had already used the money to order the necessary supplies for mending the barn roof!

Will gave a shake of his head. 'I don't want the money back. I'm comfortable here, I would rather stay.'

'But we don't want you here,' March protested.

'*You* don't want me here,' he acknowledged evenly. 'But does May feel the same way?'

March felt her frustration with this situation rise to an almost unbearable pitch. 'May will agree with whatever I decide,' she told him angrily.

'Will she?' he mused calmly. 'Why don't we stroll across to the farmhouse and ask her?' He made a move towards the door.

'How dare you?' she attacked furiously, not at all

sure, after what May had said earlier, that her sister would agree with her asking Will to leave. 'You wheedled your way in here under false pretences, charming my older sister along the way—'

'But not you,' he accepted heavily as he turned back to face her. 'March, I didn't wheedle my way in anywhere,' he rasped. 'Neither did I set out to charm anyone. I told you from the first that I was in the area on business—'

'Without telling me what that business was!' she reminded him accusingly.

'Because at the time I had no idea it *was* any of your business!' he came back harshly. 'In fact, I'm still not sure that it is. Look, March, I know you aren't going to believe me,' he continued heavily as she got ready to burst into fresh anger, 'but until you arrived back from work yesterday and announced yourself as one of the Calendar sisters, I had no idea that's who you were! Why should I have known?' he reasoned impatiently at her sceptical look.

Indeed, why should he? Unless he had found out all about the Calendar sisters before coming to the area. Which, in his place, she most certainly would have done!

She didn't believe a word he was saying, Will realized frustratedly. Not that, in the circumstances, he could altogether blame her. But no matter what she might think to the contrary, he knew he was telling her the truth.

Of course, in a fair world, he should have told both sisters, as soon as he'd realized who they were, exactly who he was, and what he was doing here. But in view of Max's recent defection—something Jude, when Will had spoken to the other man on the telephone the previous evening, had been absolutely incredulous about—

and the sisters' obvious fury towards the absent Jude Marshall, there just hadn't been the right opportunity to tell them that he was also in the area on the other man's behalf.

Besides, Will inwardly mocked himself, by the time he had learnt exactly who May and March were—but especially March!—it had been already too late to tell them the truth. Too late for him. Because by that time he'd already known himself to be so attracted to March he hadn't wanted to see the laughter and fun in her eyes replaced by scorn and dislike when told the reason he was in the area.

The same scorn and dislike he could see in those beautiful grey-green eyes at this very moment...!

He gave a heavy sigh. 'I'm sorry, March, but I'm not going anywhere.'

She glared across the room at him. 'You aren't staying here,' she told him just as determinedly.

Who would believe, looking at the two of them now, that minutes ago they had been in each other's arms, with only one obvious conclusion to their roused passions?

March had been like liquid velvet in his arms, arousing a desire in Will so strong that he still ached at the memory of it.

'I'm afraid that I am,' he came back evenly.

She gave him an impatient frown. 'But why? Why do you have to stay here? There are any number of places quite near here that I could recommend—'

'You don't live at any of them,' Will cut in ruefully.

'Me?' She looked startled now, that surprised expression as quickly turning to one of suspicion. 'Why should it matter to you where I live?' She eyed him warily.

Will gave a humourless smile. 'You can ask that, after what just happened between us?'

Her eyes seemed to shoot green sparks at being reminded of what had just happened between them. 'Nothing happened between us!' she scorned dismissively. 'Nothing of any importance, anyway,' she added insultingly.

Deliberately so, Will knew. Even in the short time he had come to know her, Will knew that anger and scorn were March's methods of defence. A defence to hide the warm softness of her nature, the vulnerability of her heart...

'Maybe not to you,' he allowed gently, doubting that it was true—he didn't believe for a moment that March was the sort of woman who went around kissing, and caressing, men she didn't care about—but not wanting to say anything that was going to hurt her. Hurting March Calendar, he was discovering, was something he never wanted to do...

'Or to you, either,' she instantly derided.

March wasn't in the mood to listen to him, Will knew, but he didn't go around kissing and caressing women he didn't care about, either...

He gave a rueful shrug. 'I doubt there is anything I could say to you right now that would convince you otherwise—'

'You're right—there isn't!' she came back scornfully. 'It really would be better, for everyone,' she added firmly, 'if you were to leave.'

Not for him it wouldn't. He liked the Calendar sisters, both of them, although that feeling went a little further where March was concerned. The last thing he wanted to do was hurt either May or March by what he was doing.

'You just don't see it, do you, March?' He gave an impatient shake of his head at her continued mulishness. 'Here you have the ideal opportunity to have some sort of say in the design of Jude's hotel and country club, by having the architect living on your own doorstep, and you want to throw away that opportunity through what I can only describe as prejudice—'

'Prejudice!' she repeated incredulously. 'Don't you understand, Mr Davenport, that we don't *want* the hotel and country club here at all—' She broke off as Will shook his head. 'What?' she prompted tautly.

'That just isn't going to happen, March,' he reasoned lightly. 'Jude is a businessman. A successful one. And he isn't going to back off on this just because of a bit of local opposition—'

'It's more than a bit,' March assured him angrily.

Will gave a grimace of frustration at her continued blinkered opinion.

'The preliminary proposal for the hotel and country club has already been approved by the local planning people. I'm just here—'

'To put the finishing touches to it,' March finished heatedly.

'In a word—yes,' he confirmed ruefully. 'March—'

'You aren't going to convince me,' she cut in determinedly. 'This is farming land. Has been farming land for generations—'

'Successfully so?' he put in softly, knowing by the way the sisters lived, the necessity for at least two of them to have jobs outside of the farm, that it wasn't even enough to support the three of them.

But he regretted his gentle prompting almost as soon as he had made it, March's face paling, eyes suddenly huge, her whole demeanour one of deflation now.

But he knew it was extremely difficult nowadays for small farms like this one to make enough just to subsist, only the larger, more modern farms that had been turned into a commercial concern managing to survive. It wasn't fair. Meant that more and more of these small farms simply went to the wall. No, it wasn't fair, it just happened to be a fact of life. No matter how much March might try to fight against it.

'Jude is offering you a more than fair price for this land, March—'

'Only so that he can make millions out of it once it's been absorbed into the rest of the estate!' she came back scathingly.

Will gave a rueful shrug of his shoulders. Of course Jude was intending to make money out of his latest venture; as Will had already said, Jude was a businessman. And Jude hadn't become as successful as he was by being delicate about it.

'It's very difficult to stop a moving train going at full speed,' he pointed out regretfully; Jude had been moving at high speed ever since Will had known him.

'Really?' March challenged derisively. 'The odd obstruction on the track seems to be effective!'

Will frowned. It was true that Jude couldn't force the Calendar sisters into selling their farm. But Will knew it was also true that Jude could make things very difficult for the sisters if he chose to do so. He knew, because he had checked this afternoon. The Calendar farm was in the middle of the estate the other man had just bought, their utilities were provided across the land Jude now owned, meaning he had the upper hand...

Unless...

'If you're really determined not to sell—'

'We are,' she snapped.

'The why don't you work with me on this rather than against Jude?' he reasoned patiently.

That suspicion was back in her gaze. 'I don't understand what you mean by working with you.'

Neither did he, not really. The idea had only occurred to him as they were talking. Surely there must be a way for this to work out so that no one was hurt in the process, a way for the sisters to keep their farm, but to keep Jude happy at the same time. Most of all, Will knew, he wanted to stop March continuing to look at him in that scornful, suspicious way!

'I'm not sure myself yet,' he admitted self-derisively. 'But there has to be a way.'

Her mouth twisted scornfully. 'Well, when you think of it, let me know. In the meantime—'

'I'm staying put,' he cut in determinedly.

She gave him a disgusted look. 'Please yourself,' she bit out dismissively. 'But don't expect any more invitations to dinner,' she added tartly as she reached for the door-handle.

As a parting shot, it was pretty weak, and they both knew it, Will giving March a rueful smile. 'I still owe the two of you dinner,' he reminded lightly.

'And I'm sure May would enjoy that,' she came back tartly.

'But not you,' he acknowledged dryly.

'As far as I'm concerned, eating with the enemy is as bad as sleeping with them,' March snapped—and as instantly regretted it if the colour that flooded her cheeks was anything to go by. 'I meant—'

'I know what you meant, March,' Will assured her laughingly. 'And let me assure you—I do not want to ''sleep'' with you.' He moved to open the door for her. 'Nor,' he added huskily, 'do I consider you an enemy.'

They were standing only inches apart now, Will very conscious of the warmth of March's body, the heady perfume she wore, the light dusting of freckles across the bridge of her nose, the pouting perfection of her mouth.

He also knew that if she didn't soon get out of here he was going to kiss her again!

As if aware of the impulse, March moved outside onto the top of the stairs. 'The sentiment isn't reciprocated,' she told him waspishly. 'And next time you speak to Jude Marshall...'

'Yes?' he prompted warily.

She gave a humourless smile. 'Tell him to come and fight his own battles—we're sick of dealing with his minions!' she added insultingly.

An insult Will had no intention of responding to! 'I'll tell him.' He nodded.

Although he doubted the challenge would mean too much to the other man; as far as he could tell, Jude was otherwise occupied at the moment with the attractions of the actress April Robine!

March gave him a sharp look before clattering down the metal steps and moving lightly across the frozen yard to the farmhouse.

Will watched her every step of the way, admiring the coltish grace with which she moved; long-legged, her youthful energy dented by their conversation but not diminished.

He closed the door slowly behind him as he moved back into the warmth of the studio. Apart from that time he had held March in his arms, it hadn't been a very successful encounter.

Apart from—!

He was quickly discovering that the only thing that

did mean anything was holding March, kissing and caressing her!

He closed his eyes, easily conjuring up the feel of March, her warmth, the passion he knew they had shared. He wanted March Calendar, found her mercurial changes of mood fascinating, her seductive beauty affecting him as no other woman ever had.

But, at the same time, his desire for March only made this situation more complicated.

Impossibly so…?

CHAPTER SEVEN

'FLYING a little high with your friend in the Ferrari, aren't you, March?' Clive taunted sarcastically as March placed a mug of coffee down on his desk.

Making the hot drinks throughout the day was apparently also the job of the receptionist, March had learnt shortly after starting work here two years ago. In fact, after only a few weeks' employment March had been amazed at the amount of jobs that came under that title.

If truth were known, Clive and Michelle were just too mean to employ anyone else, preferring to leave all the little incidental jobs to March rather than employ an office junior. After all, it would cut into their profit!

March innocently returned Clive's mocking gaze as she stepped back from his desk. 'I didn't know Ferraris could fly,' she easily returned his sarcasm.

She had never found working for Clive to be easy, and over the last few months, as his flirtatious attitude had increased whenever Michelle hadn't been around, she had found it even harder; obviously Will Davenport's appearance yesterday wasn't going to make that particular situation any easier!

'Very funny,' Clive sneered humourlessly. 'You—'

'Stop teasing her, Clive,' Michelle cut in with light rebuke in the gentle softness of her voice. 'Clive was saying last night that you have a new boyfriend, March.' She turned to her interestedly.

March had never been able to understand how two such different people could not only work together but have lived together for the last ten years too. Where Clive was brash and outspoken, Michelle was quiet and considerate. Where Clive had screen-star good looks, Michelle's were rather mousy, with her light brown hair and brown eyes, her features tending to be a little plain unless animated.

A definite attraction of opposites, March had dismissed uninterestedly after a couple of months of working here; Michelle was probably completely overwhelmed by the fact that a good-looking man like Clive was interested in her, and Clive, as March had come to know only too well, probably thrived as the more attractive of the pair. He certainly liked to feel that every woman in the vicinity found him irresistible, and any woman that didn't quickly became the target of his sharp tongue.

Which included March!

After only two weeks of working in the agency, the needed money aside, March could quite happily have given in her notice. But the gentler Michelle was so much the opposite, so appreciative of everything that March did, that she hadn't liked to let the other woman down by leaving. Luckily it didn't happen too often that she was left alone with Clive in the office, and he usually behaved himself when Michelle was around.

'What's he like?' Michelle prompted interestedly, brown eyes glowing warmly as March gave her a cup of tea.

'Will isn't my boyfriend,' March dismissed, not quite meeting the other woman's gaze. 'I—he—he's a family friend,' she hastily invented—well, he was apparently a friend of Max's, and as Max was almost a member of her family...! 'He's just staying with us for a couple of weeks,' she added dismissively.

Which reminded her, she would have to deal with the paperwork of acquiring a rentee for two weeks through Carter and Jones.

'Yesterday's kiss didn't just look friendly to me,' Clive put in speculatively.

March eyed him coolly. 'Well, I can assure you that it was.' Damn Will for having kissed her in front of Clive in that possessive way!

Admittedly, at the time she had been quite grateful for his proprietary attitude, but not if it was going to make Clive more unbearable to work with than usual.

'Any more news about the Hanworth Estate, March?' Michelle changed the subject with ease.

Although it wasn't really much of a change now that March knew that Will was Jude Marshall's architect!

'Not really.' She grimaced, warming to Michelle for her concern; it had been Michelle who had initially told her what Jude Marshall's intentions were for the neighbouring Hanworth Estate. 'I suppose we will just have to wait and see.'

'Personally, I think you and your sisters are idiots for not selling,' Clive told her disgustedly. 'The man must be offering way over the odds, for a farm that is virtually worthless.'

March felt the rage building within her at this man's complete lack of sensitivity, her eyes sparkling, bright spots of angry colour in her cheeks. 'It isn't worthless to me—'

'I'm sure Clive didn't mean to be unkind,' Michelle put in apologetically. 'It's your home, of course it isn't worthless to you. It's just such a pity that it's in the middle of the Hanworth land,' she added sympathetically.

'A pity' wasn't quite the phrase March would have used! 'I—'

'Good morning!' greeted a cheerful voice that made March stiffen with recognition. 'I wondered if you were free for an early lunch, March?' Will Davenport prompted lightly as he came into the agency.

March slowly turned to face him, unable to hide her amazement at this man's cheek. They hadn't parted on good terms at all last night, and she was sure she had made her feelings completely clear about ever seeing him again. And yet here he was, cheerfully offering to buy her lunch as if the two of them were the best of friends.

And, after what she had said to Clive and Michelle earlier, that was exactly what the other couple thought that they were!

'Go ahead, March,' Michelle invited. 'It's almost twelve o'clock anyway.' She smiled encouragingly after giving Will an appreciative glance.

Michelle obviously had a weakness for good-looking men, March decided disgruntledly, grudgingly acknowledging that Will did look extremely handsome this morning in fitted black denims and a blue jumper the exact colour of his eyes. He was also smiling at March as if last night had never happened!

But what choice did she have but to collect her coat and handbag in preparation for going out to lunch with him? Or, at least, seeming as if she were going out to lunch with him, because once they were outside she intended telling him exactly what he could do with his lunch!

'Make sure you're back by one,' Clive told her hardly. 'I'm taking Michelle out to lunch today to celebrate our tenth anniversary,' he added derisively.

'It won't matter if you're a few minutes late,' Michelle assured March with a definite twinkle in her eye.

March accompanied Will down the street, not having spoken so much as a word to him yet. Probably because she knew that once she started talking she might not be able to stop—and none of it would have been pleasant!

She had hardly slept at all last night, for thinking of that time in Will's arms, alternating between anger that it had happened at all and a wish for it to happen again. Completely illogical, March knew, but nevertheless that was how she had felt.

It hadn't helped that May had been full of questions last night on March's return from the studio. Of course March had told her sister nothing of her time in Will Davenport's arms, only confirming that he was indeed working for Jude Marshall, as his architect. But that hadn't stopped May from speculating, especially as March had returned without the cup of sugar she had supposedly gone over there for!

'As pleasant as this change might be,' Will spoke teasingly at her side, 'are you going to remain silent all through lunch too?'

March turned to glare at him. 'I have nothing to say to you,' she snapped. 'And we aren't having lunch!' she added disgustedly.

'Oh.' He looked disappointed.

She gave an impatient sigh. 'I only left with you just now because to do anything else would have been too awkward to explain.'

'I can deal with awkward,' Will assured her. 'After all, I've been dealing with you for three days now!' he added mockingly.

'Not awkward for you,' she told him irritably, wishing

her heart would resume its normal rhythmic beat, that she wasn't so aware of the intimacies she had shared with this man the previous evening.

Although, to look at Will, that time in his arms might never have happened as he grinned at her in innocent enquiry.

'I had only just finished explaining that you're a family friend when you walked in the door,' she said exasperatedly.

'Well, that's a definite step up from being one of Jude Marshall's minions,' he acknowledged dryly.

March felt her cheeks flush as he repeated the insult she had deliberately thrown at him the previous evening. '"If the cap fits",' she bit out harshly.

'I don't think I've ever worn a cap,' Will remarked consideringly. 'Maybe when I was at junior school—'

'I didn't mean it literally,' March cut in impatiently.

He chuckled at her obvious discomfort. 'Lighten up, March,' he encouraged as she continued to scowl at him. 'May certainly didn't seem to bear any grudge when I had coffee with her this morning,' he added brightly.

'May obviously has a more forgiving nature than I do!' She gave him a glowering look, not in the least surprised that he had called at the farm to see May this morning, or that her sister had given him a cup of coffee; May just didn't seem to see this situation as March did.

May also hadn't spent any time in this man's arms, hadn't completely forgotten the farm—and everything else—as she'd been kissed and caressed by him. As she'd kissed and caressed him back!

It wasn't that she was a complete innocent—she had had boyfriends in the past, had even believed herself a little in love with one or two of them. But never before had she responded in the way she had to Will, knowing even now that she had wanted to make love with him, to lay naked in his arms as they made love to each other. That was just another reason for her to be angry with him!

'Probably,' Will accepted ruefully now. 'She had a phone call from her director while I was there; her screen test has been moved forward to tomorrow. Something to do with the star of the film being in the country next week.'

March frowned at him. 'I'm sure May is perfectly capable of telling me that herself when I get home this evening.'

He shrugged. 'Your big sister has the impression you don't approve of her proposed acting career.'

Her eyes widened. 'That's absolute rubbish!' she gasped indignantly. 'You're making that up,' she accused uncertainly.

Surely May couldn't really believe that...?

Will gave her a searching glance, knowing by her hesitant tone that she wasn't at all sure about her last claim. And with good reason, if his conversation with May this morning was anything to go by.

Max's engagement to the younger Calendar sister had obviously shaken the sisters' resolve to keep the farm, May convinced that Max, once he had completely severed his ties with Jude, would want to go to London to work, and that January would go with him. Which, Will also thought, seemed a pretty astute guess. With May's possible offer of an acting role in a film later this year, that only left March. May, he knew, was seriously considering turning down the film offer in order to support March's stand.

Which was why Will had come into town this morning and done what he had done...

Although perhaps he had better not mention that to March just yet. Wait and see what the reaction was. After all, he could just be wrong...

He had felt restless and unfocused after March had left him yesterday evening, the plans he had been working on before March had arrived offering no incentive whatsoever. Finally he had climbed up into the attic and looked at those paintings that March claimed weren't paintings at all.

They were good.

In fact, they were better than good.

So much so that Will had parcelled six of them up before coming into town to post them off to a friend of his who ran a gallery in London. As far as he could tell March no longer even looked at her own work, so there wasn't much chance of her missing half a dozen of them. And if Will's opinion of them turned out to be the correct one...

Not that he thought March would see his high-handedness that way. Which was why he had no intention of telling her what he had done until he heard back from Graham.

The matriarch of the Calendar family must have been something else, Will had decided after spending some time looking at all of March's paintings, because their father, that bluntly spoken Yorkshireman, certainly hadn't been the one to give them their array of artistic talents.

'Am I?' he gently prompted March now.

'Of course,' she scorned. 'I've done nothing but encourage May to go for this opportunity. You've heard me yourself.'

'At the same time that you're absolutely adamant you aren't going to sell the farm,' Will pointed out ruefully.

'I should have known it would all come back to that again,' March snapped disgustedly. 'Don't you ever think of anything else?' she added scathingly.

He very much doubted she would want to hear about the thoughts that had kept him from sleeping last night!

How could he have possibly slept when his mind and senses were so full of March, of how she had felt in his arms, of how much he wanted to make love with her?

'Oh, I give the odd thought to food now and again,' he answered her dismissively. 'Talking of which...'

'*You* were talking of food—I wasn't,' March came back tartly. 'I haven't eaten my sandwiches from yesterday yet—'

'Ugh, they must be disgusting by now,' Will broke in with a grimace. 'But I'm quite happy to go to a sandwich bar if you insist,' he assured her, at the same time directing her into the sandwich bar they had been about to pass. 'I'll even let you buy me lunch today, if you feel you must,' he added with soft challenge.

Hah! That had her confused, the conflicting emotions easily read on her face: of returning his gesture of yesterday, and as such not feeling beholden to him, warring with her desire to tell him what he could do with this second suggestion of lunch.

As she pushed open the door to the sandwich bar, to precede him inside, he knew the former had won. Luckily for him. Because, for the moment, he had completely run out of options for ways of spending time with March. Something he very much wanted to do.

'You know, the more I see of your boss, the less I like him,' Will told her grimly once they had sat down and ordered their sandwiches and drinks. 'He looks the sort who turns nasty if he doesn't get his own way.'

March looked at him beneath lowered lashes. 'As opposed to…?' she taunted.

He gave a decisive shake of his head at her deliberate barb. 'Nasty isn't in my nature,' he assured her dryly. 'Determination. Arrogance, maybe—'

'Maybe?' she repeated with a derisive snort.

'If warranted,' he acknowledged laughingly. 'But nasty? No, I don't think that's part of my nature at all.' He gave another shake of his head.

March looked at him unblinkingly for several minutes, before slowly relaxing, her smile rueful. 'No, I don't think it is either,' she conceded wryly.

'Thank you.' Will gave a gracious inclination of his head. 'Does Carter have anything to do with the questions you were asking me yesterday concerning undervaluing property?'

The return to his original subject was done so suddenly that March didn't even have time to try to hide her consternation—even if she could have done, which was doubtful!—looking across at him frowningly now.

'Add sneaky to determined and arrogant,' she bit out tersely.

He shrugged unapologetically. 'Does he?'

March's gaze no longer met his; she was obviously perfectly aware of how easily readable her emotions were. 'They were merely abstract questions,' she dismissed huskily. 'Not specifically aimed at anyone,' she added firmly.

'Add evasive to your other list of attractions,' Will returned dryly.

She raised dark brows, a smile now lurking at the

corners of her kissable mouth. 'Do I have a list of "attractions"?' she prompted teasingly.

'Oh, yes,' Will confirmed appreciatively, knowing she was deliberately changing the subject, but at this moment willing to let her do so. 'Would you like me to tell you what they are?' He quirked blond brows at her suggestively.

'Er—no,' she decided hastily, leaning back as their food and drinks arrived, obviously relieved at the interruption.

Not that he could blame her; it could prove highly embarrassing if he were to start talking about all March's wonderful attributes. Besides, this was hardly the time or the place...

Now that he was here with March, having lunch with her, despite her obvious reluctance, he was beginning to feel a slight trepidation about sending those paintings off to London. Last night it had all seemed so simple: send the paintings to Graham and await his artistic criticism. But here and now, with March sitting only inches away from him, he wasn't so sure of his actions.

Of course, it would all be easier if Graham were to agree with March's own opinion of her artistic talent, but if Graham agreed with Will, then he was going to have to talk to March about them, and what he had done. Looking at her now, knowing how hard it was to get past her prickly nature, he knew that wasn't going to be an easy matter!

'Is the sandwich not to your liking? You were frowning,' March explained at his questioning look. 'We can always swap if you want to; I'll be perfectly happy with the tuna if you would like my egg mayonnaise,' she offered lightly.

'''Greater love hath no man—'' or woman, and all that?' He grinned.

'It's just a sandwich, Will,' she said dryly.

His grin widened. 'You're fun to be with, do you know that?'

'What does that have to do with exchanging sandwiches?' she came back tartly—although there was a slight flush of pleasure in her cheeks now.

'The tuna is fine,' he dismissed. 'But I'm glad I'm back to being Will; ''Mr Davenport'' sounds like it should be my father you're talking to.' He grimaced.

'You have parents?' March prompted interestedly.

Will burst out laughing. 'Did you think I was manufactured?' he teased at her puzzled expression.

She gave him a scathing grimace. 'I meant, are your parents still alive?'

'Well, they were the last time I spoke to them.' He nodded. 'Which was only last week. Dad's a retired doctor,' he continued hastily as he sensed March was about to give him another cutting reply. 'My mother was a nurse.'

'A hospital romance,' March mused.

'I don't know—I've never asked them.' Will shrugged ruefully.

'Oh, the disinterest of youth,' she reproved mockingly.

'Unless I'm mistaken, young lady, I'm several years older than you,' he said dryly.

'Almost Methuselah.' She nodded, grey-green eyes glowing with laughter.

'Well, I wouldn't go that far!' He grimaced. 'Do you have anything against older men?'

'Do you have anything against younger women?' she came back tartly, the colour in her cheeks now owing nothing to pleasure as she merely looked embarrassed by the intimate turn the conversation had taken.

'In this particular case—no.' He smiled warmly, perfectly happy with the conversation himself.

March swallowed hard, her gaze once again avoiding his as she took a sip of her coffee. 'Isn't it strange that your parents were both medical people, and yet you became an architect?' she abruptly changed the subject back to his parents.

'Not really—I faint at the first sight of blood!' he admitted with a self-conscious grimace.

March looked astounded for several seconds, and then she burst out laughing, her eyes glowing, two tiny dimples appearing endearingly either side of that smiling mouth.

She continued to chuckle, giving Will chance to enjoy her laughter. Even if it was at his expense! Not that he minded that at all if it meant he could see March smiling.

'Feet of clay?' he finally prompted ruefully.

'Not really.' She shook her head, still smiling. 'I was just thinking how useless you would be on a farm. It's a busy time of year for us. Most of the ewes have already lambed, and we will have the cows calving shortly. But at least I know where not to come for help if there are any complications!' she added teasingly.

'Not unless you want to step over me during the process,' he confirmed lightly.

'I think we'll pass, if you don't mind,' she said dryly, her eyes widening as she glanced down at her wristwatch. 'It's almost one o'clock, I'll have to be getting back.'

Was there a slight note of regret in her voice, or was it just wishful thinking on his part? Probably the latter, he decided, but one could dream, couldn't one?

'One of your bosses at least said you didn't have to hurry back,' he reminded her. 'And you haven't finished your sandwich yet,' he pointed out practically.

'I'm really not that hungry.' March pushed away the plate containing the half-eaten sandwich, taking a last gulp of her coffee before standing up. 'Some of us have work to go to, you know,' she added with a return of her usual tartness, before moving across to the counter to pay for their lunch.

Will let her, knowing it was a pride thing on her part, and having no wish to upset her any more than he already had. Besides, it gave him chance to watch her, to admire the gentle sway of her hips, the silky length of her legs.

Although he wasn't quite so pleased to note that several other men in the room were doing the same thing! But March, to give her her due, seemed completely unaware of the male admiration coming in her direction, looking to neither left nor right as she moved through the room to join Will at the door.

'I may faint at the sight of blood,' Will told her quietly as they moved off down the street together, 'but otherwise I'm pretty good in a crisis. If you should ever need any help,' he added huskily.

March gave him a searching sideways glance. 'I'll bear that in mind,' she finally answered softly.

Will wasn't at all sure what was going on in the estate agency of Carter and Jones, but he was pretty sure that something was. He was equally sure, no matter how evasive she might have been on the subject earlier, that March knew there was too. And Will had meant what he said about Clive Carter; the other man looked as if he might turn nasty if thwarted.

But having offered his help, with March as prickly as

she was, Will knew he couldn't do any more for the moment.

But that didn't mean he didn't intend keeping an eye on the situation, if only from a distance...

CHAPTER EIGHT

MARCH had no intention of telling May of her second lunch with Will, but the two of them had watched the news together, eaten dinner, and still her sister hadn't mentioned the telephone call she had received from the film director earlier that day.

Quite how to approach the subject, without mentioning having lunch with Will, March didn't know. Although she had certainly taken to heart Will's earlier comments about May's reluctance to even go to London for the screen test. And the reason for it!

'Anything interesting happen today?' she attempted casually as the two of them strolled over to the barn where they were keeping the ewes with their more delicate lambs.

May gave her a puzzled glance. 'I told you earlier, I've been at the farm all day.'

March nodded. 'But no visitors? Telephone calls?' A casual glance in the direction of the studio showed it to be in darkness, which meant that Will wasn't home yet. Or he had been home and gone out again. Which was interesting, because she didn't think he knew anyone else in the area...

'I haven't heard from January, if that's what you're wondering,' May assured her lightly as the two of them entered the warmth of the lambing shed. 'But then, I wouldn't expect to. Would you?' she added mischievously as she strolled over to the ewe in the first pen. 'Hello, Ginny, aren't you a clever girl?' she soothed, at the same time running a critical eye over the animal still awaiting the arrival of her offspring.

Their father had always deplored the way the three girls gave each of their animals a name, sure that making pets of the animals would only make it harder for them all when it came time for them to 'go to market', as he delicately put it. That might have been true when they were younger, but as the sisters had grown older, they had come to accept the simplicity of farming life, the cows and sheep going to market for sale, for whatever reason.

Although that wasn't quite the case with Ginny, the ewe having become a firm favourite with all the sisters over the years. She was probably approaching the end of her usefulness now, but all of them were loath to make that decision.

But March really wasn't interested in Ginny, or any other of their livestock, at this particular moment. 'I wasn't actually referring to January,' she prompted tautly.

May gave her a searching glance now. 'Will popped over for a cup of coffee this morning, if that's what you want to know.' She shrugged.

Well, it was a start!

'What did he want?' she bit out abruptly.

'I told you, a cup of coffee. Oh, and he brought back the cup of sugar you went over there to borrow last night,' her sister added teasingly.

March felt the colour in her cheeks as she remembered the reason for her hurried departure from the studio the previous evening. 'Good of him,' she snapped.

May laughed softly. 'You weren't exactly subtle, were you?' She gave an exasperated shake of her head. 'Will didn't say too much about it, but I'm sure you gave him a hard time of it last night once you knew who he was.'

That wasn't quite the way March would have put what had happened between herself and Will the previous evening!

Her gaze was evasive. 'I told you he was a snake in the grass!'

May gave a heavy sigh. 'He's simply doing his job, March, in the best way he knows how. Like all of us,' she added quietly.

'Is that what he told you?' she scorned. 'I happen to think differently.' She gave a dismissive shake of her head, not having missed her sister's second husky remark, and not about to be sidetracked by talk of Will Davenport, either; she had heard far too much from him today already! 'May, how do you really feel about letting all of this go?' She opened her arms expansively, deliberately keeping her own expression neutral.

May had always done what was best for all three sisters, without complaint, without regrets, as far as March knew. But March simply couldn't believe that concerning May's hesitation about the offered screen test, clearly remembering how excited her sister had been after the director had first approached her.

Much as March would hate letting Jude Marshall have his own way where their farm was concerned, she wasn't about to stand in her sister's way, either.

'Well, we aren't going to sell it, are we?' May answered brightly. 'So that possibility doesn't even arise.'

'But—'

'Good evening, ladies,' Will greeted smoothly as he stood in the doorway to the lambing shed. 'None about to give birth, I hope?' He held back cautiously.

'Not right this minute, no,' March answered him dryly

OFFICIAL OPINION POLL

ANSWER 3 QUESTIONS AND WE'LL SEND YOU
2 FREE BOOKS AND A FREE GIFT!

0074823 ‖‖▮‖‖‖▮ ‖‖▮‖‖ ‖▮‖‖   FREE GIFT CLAIM # | 3953

YOUR OPINION COUNTS!

Please check TRUE or FALSE below to express your opinion about the following statements:

Q1 Do you believe in "true love"?

"TRUE LOVE HAPPENS ONLY ONCE IN A LIFETIME."
○ TRUE
○ FALSE

Q2 Do you think marriage has any value in today's world?

"YOU CAN BE TOTALLY COMMITTED TO SOMEONE WITHOUT BEING MARRIED."
○ TRUE
○ FALSE

Q3 What kind of books do you enjoy?

"A GREAT NOVEL MUST HAVE A HAPPY ENDING."
○ TRUE
○ FALSE

YES, I have scratched the area below.

Please send me the 2 **FREE BOOKS** and **FREE GIFT** for which I qualify. I understand I am under no obligation to purchase any books, as explained on the back of this card.

DETACH AND MAIL CARD TODAY!

306 HDL DZ35   106 HDL DZ4L

(H-P-03/04)

FIRST NAME   LAST NAME

ADDRESS

APT.#   CITY

STATE/PROV.   ZIP/POSTAL CODE

www.eHarlequin.com

before turning to give her sister a knowing smile. 'Will goes green at the sight of blood,' she informed May derisively.

'I believe that was "faints at the sight of blood",' he corrected with a grimace.

May nodded. 'March has the same reaction to spiders.' She shot March a mischievous smile.

'Really?' Will's sky-blue gaze was turned on her mockingly now. 'You didn't tell me that.'

'You didn't ask me!' March came back tartly. He was still wearing the blue jumper and black denims, so perhaps he hadn't been home and then out again, after all...

'So I didn't.' He chuckled in acknowledgement. 'So what are the two of you doing out here if you aren't assisting in a birth?' he prompted interestedly.

'Checking that there isn't one taking place,' March answered him impatiently; she had finally been getting somewhere with her conversation with May, could quite well have done without this interruption. Especially from Will!

He nodded, obviously no more informed about the workings of their farm than he had been a few minutes ago. 'I've just come back from town—anyone feel like joining me in a glass of wine?'

'No, thanks—'

'Lovely—'

Both sisters had answered at once, March in the negative—obviously! May in the positive.

'Two to one against, March,' Will informed her triumphantly. 'The wine wins!'

Her gaze narrowed. He was looking decidedly pleased with himself this evening. Very much as if he knew something they didn't...

'Okay,' she conceded lightly, earning herself a searching glance from Will now as he puzzled over the possible reason for her easy acquiescence.

Oh, well, a puzzled Will Davenport had to be preferable to a knowing one!

'Your place or mine?' he prompted once they were outside in the crisp night air.

March shot him a pitying glance for his facetiousness, receiving a wide-eyed innocent look in return that didn't fool her for a minute. 'Ours,' she answered flatly. 'It's warmer,' she added by way of explanation as he raised questioning brows.

'Really?' He shrugged. 'Obviously I've been out all day, but I've found the heat in the studio in the evenings more than adequate so far.' He gave her a challenging look.

A look March returned with obvious irritation. If he were hoping to embarrass her by covert references to yesterday evening, then he was going to be out of luck; she had more important things on her mind this evening—such as May's screen test tomorrow. Or not...as the case may be.

'You—'

'There's more room in the farmhouse,' May put in briskly. 'We'll go and get out the glasses while you collect the bottle of wine.' She looped her arm firmly through March's in order to pull her towards the kitchen door. 'What's going on?' she hissed softly.

'Going on?' March delayed lightly. 'Why, nothing.' She gave a definite shake of her head.

May gave her a reproving look as the two of them entered the warmth of the kitchen, that look turning to one of narrow-eyed searching as the sudden silence in the kitchen became overwhelming. At least, it seemed so to March!

What could her sister see in her face? What emotion was it giving away now?

'Not another one!' May finally gasped incredulously.

'What?' She frowned, her hands turning into fists at her sides as she tried to withstand that penetrating look from May.

'I don't believe it.' May shook her head dazedly. 'How on earth did that happen? The man's only been here a couple of days!'

March gave an impatient snort as she shook her head. 'I have no idea what you're talking about,' she dismissed impatiently, reaching up into the cupboard to take out the wineglasses. As May obviously wasn't going to!

'You're in love with Will Davenport,' May stated shakily.

March had turned so sharply at her sister's statement that one of the glasses slipped out of her hand and shattered on the tiled floor. Unnoticed by either of them, it seemed.

May simply stared at March disbelievingly, obviously deeply shaken by her own observation.

As for March—shaken didn't even begin to describe how she felt!

In love with Will Davenport?

She couldn't be!

'Here we are—' Will broke off his cheery greeting as he entered the kitchen and saw the two sisters simply staring at each other, both of them pale as magnolias.

A smashed glass lay on the floor between them, and yet it didn't seem as if one of them had thrown it at the other, no anger burning in either of their faces—in fact they both looked more shocked than angry.

Will had no idea what could have taken place between

the two sisters in the short time he had been gone—but something certainly had! May was staring at March in complete disbelief, and March was staring at him in exactly the same manner.

May was the first to recover, seeming to shake herself slightly as she turned to face him. 'Sorry.' She gave the ghost of a smile. 'We were—um—discussing farm business,' she dismissed evasively.

And untruthfully, if Will were any judge of character; March was the more easily readable of the sisters, but May was definitely the more honest. And she wasn't being honest now.

'Someone seems to have had an accident,' he pointed out lightly, glancing down at the broken glass that lay on the floor between the two sisters.

'That was me,' March acknowledged shakily, her face turned away, her hair falling forward to shield her expression as she went down on her haunches to begin picking up the shattered glass.

'Not like that!' Will moved quickly, grabbing her wrist to pull her back to her feet. 'You'll cut yourself—' He broke off as he discovered he was already too late in his warning, March even now pulling a sliver of the glass from one of her fingers, blood instantly welling from the cut it left.

She looked up sharply, her gaze glitteringly hard as she looked at him challengingly. 'Aren't you going to faint?' she bit out harshly.

Strangely enough, no. Perhaps it was only the sight of blood in the abstract, when the person was unknown to him, only the blood seeming real. But he knew he wasn't going to faint at the sight of March's blood, that he only wanted to do something to stop the bleeding, to take away the pain for her if he could.

'Here.' May was the one to hand him a clean cloth.

Will took it, hesitating before wrapping it about her finger. 'Is all the glass out?' he rasped as March winced.

'Don't fuss, Will!' she snapped, at the same time pulling her hand out of his grasp. 'I already have two mother hens in May and January, I don't need a third one!' she added nastily.

'March!' May gasped, obviously scandalized.

'Why don't the two of you just leave me alone?' March cried, eyes blazing angrily, before she turned and ran from the room.

Will looked at May, noting the paleness of her cheeks, the unshed tears swimming in huge green eyes.

May looked back at him concernedly, letting him know that he probably didn't look much better than she did!

'Was it something I said?' he finally murmured ruefully.

May gave a shaky smile. 'No—I think it may have been something *I* said!' She grimaced.

Also the reason for the tension between the two sisters when he'd first entered the kitchen…?

He glanced across to the door that led out to the hallway. 'Should I go up and see if she's okay?'

May actually chuckled. 'Not if you value your life!' She gave a rueful shake of her head. 'Leave it a while; she'll come back down when she's ready,' she advised as she took the wine from him and deftly opened the bottle. 'March is quick to anger, but just as quick to calm down again. Especially when she knows she's the one in the wrong,' she added huskily.

'But—'

'Have some wine, Will,' May told him briskly, pouring it out into the two glasses that had remained intact. 'You'll see, March will come back down soon.'

There didn't seem to be too much chance of that during the next hour as the two of them sat in the kitchen after clearing up the broken glass, talking quietly, slowly emptying the bottle of wine.

They had heard March moving around upstairs once or twice, probably to the bathroom to deal with the cut on her finger, but other than that there was no sign of her.

'I'm sorry about this, Will,' May finally sighed an hour later. 'It's all my fault, and I'm sure it isn't me you want to be sitting here drinking wine with!' she added ruefully.

Will gave her a considering look. 'It isn't?'

'We both know that it isn't.' She laughed, her gaze gently reproving.

His gaze narrowed. 'Do we?'

'Don't you start!' May warned dryly, putting down her wineglass decisively. 'I think I'll just go up and check that she's okay.' She stood up.

'Maybe I should leave—'

'Not on my account, I hope,' March dismissed lightly as she came into the kitchen.

Will looked at her searchingly. Whatever May had said or done earlier to upset March, the latter now had that response very firmly under control. In fact, for once, her expression was totally unreadable!

'I'm just on my way out, anyway,' March continued brightly, reaching for a jacket from behind the kitchen door. 'I told Aunt Lyn that I would go over one evening this week and help her to move all the wedding presents over to Sara and Josh's cottage before they come back from their honeymoon next week,' she added briskly.

'Our cousin Sara was married last weekend,' May took the time to explain to Will. 'And I thought we *both* promised to go over and help.' May looked at her sister frowningly.

March flicked back her long hair. 'Well, as you're obviously busy this evening...'

Will stood up abruptly. 'I was just leaving—'

'No, you weren't—'

'There's absolutely no need for you to do that,' March cut firmly across her sister's protest. 'It doesn't need both of us, May,' she insisted impatiently. 'I won't be long. You stay here and keep Will company.' She gave him a cold glance.

Will couldn't even begin to guess what had caused this rift between the two sisters, but he hoped that it had nothing to do with him. Or his reason for being here.

'No, I really must be going.' He drained his glass with one swallow. 'I have some work to do myself this evening, anyway,' he assured May dismissively.

'That will certainly make a change,' March came back crisply. 'Jude Marshall probably wonders what he's paying you for!'

May simply stared at her sister in embarrassed dismay, obviously having given up, for the moment, on trying to curb March's rudeness.

Will counted to ten before answering her; losing his own temper, something he rarely did anyway, would not help the situation. 'As it happens, he hasn't paid me anything yet.' He kept his voice deliberately even. 'I only get paid when I produce the finished article.'

'Then you had better get on with it, hadn't you?' March bit out scathingly.

He counted to twenty this time, not sure that even that was going to be enough to stop the sharp reply he wanted to give her. He had never met anyone, male or female, who could be as outspokenly rude as March Calendar.

He gave an acknowledging inclination of his head, blue gaze narrowed. 'I intend to.'

Maybe, after all, the best thing for all of them would be for him to remove his presence from the farm as quickly as possible; the last thing he wanted to do was be the cause of a lasting friction between the two sisters.

If, indeed, he was the cause. Which he wasn't sure of. But it was enough that he now felt extremely uncomfortable in their presence. 'Have a good evening,' he told May—more out of hope than a belief that she would, deciding it was best not to try and say anything else to March this evening.

She might be quick to anger, and quick to calm down again, but at the moment that certainly wasn't in evidence!

May walked him to the door, standing outside on the step. 'I'm really sorry about this, Will,' she told him huskily, shaking her head regretfully.

'Don't be,' he assured her. 'It's you I feel sorry for,' he added with feeling.

She chuckled softly. 'Then don't,' she assured him with a smile. 'March is only angry because she knows she's the one in the wrong.'

He raised blond brows. 'You would never know it to look at her!'

'But I know March, you see,' May added softly. 'That's the real problem,' she said enigmatically.

It was just too complex for Will to even begin to work out. If he wanted to. And he wasn't sure that he did. Oh, he still found March the most beautiful and fascinating woman he had ever met, but he hardly knew her in this coldly sarcastic mood, certainly couldn't tell what she was thinking or feeling. And without that, she was merely a beautiful enigma...

'Rather you than me!' he told May with feeling, raising a hand in parting as he walked briskly across to the studio without a backward glance.

What on earth could May have said or done to March to cause her to behave in that uncharacteristic way?

He simply didn't know. From the little May had said on the subject, she wasn't about to tell him, either. And it was a sure fact that March wasn't going to!

CHAPTER NINE

'MARCH—'

'I do not wish to discuss it!' she cut in sharply on May's tentative attempt to breach the strained silence between them once Will had left. 'Other than to say that you're totally wrong,' she added hardly—totally nullifying her previous statement!

'Am I?'

'Yes!' Her eyes flashed, her face pale. 'I am not in love with Will Davenport!'

Yet...

Because she was very much afraid that, until May had made the observation earlier, she had been well on her way to being just that!

She certainly responded to him in a way she never had with any other man. She also quite enjoyed the verbal sparring that went on between them. And there was no denying that her heart gave a jolt every time she saw him.

But that wasn't necessarily love, was it? Sexual attraction. Sexual awareness. But not love.

Because she refused to be in love with a man who was so closely associated with Jude Marshall!

January might have fallen into that trap, and Max, in his wisdom, had decided that it was better for all concerned if he severed his business ties with Jude Marshall. But that didn't mean any relationship March had with Will would turn out the same way. And she refused to even consider anything less.

As such she refused to love Will Davenport!

'You can't choose whether or not to love someone, March.' May's gentle rebuke told March that she must have actually spoken those last words out loud.

She blinked, a little disconcerted at having expressed her feelings so openly. 'Of course you can. I just did,' she dismissed briskly. 'Now are you coming with me to Aunt Lyn's or not?' she prompted abruptly.

'I am,' May conceded dryly. 'But let me have a look at that finger first, hmm?'

March looked across at her sister in exasperation, that exasperation quickly turning to affection as May looked back at her teasingly.

March stepped forward, all the tension going out of her as she gave her sister a hug. 'I do love you, May.' She chuckled ruefully.

'I love you too,' May returned huskily. 'Which is why I don't want you to make yourself unhappy about this situation. It worked out okay for January, why shouldn't it work out for you and—?'

'I'll make a deal with you, May,' she cut in dryly. 'You don't mention Will again this evening, and I'll take care of the farm over the weekend while you go down to London for the screen test.' She gave May a knowing look as her sister gave a surprised gasp. 'I told you he was a snake in the grass!' she added mischievously.

'Will told you?' May frowned. 'But how—when—?'

'Never mind the how or when,' March dismissed briskly. 'Give this director a call before we go out and tell him you'll be there some time tomorrow.'

'But—'

'No buts, May. What's good advice for me also applies to you,' she stated firmly. 'The complication of whether or not we keep or sell the farm can take care of itself for the moment. You have to at least go for the screen test, May,' she reasoned persuasively. 'You'll never forgive yourself if you don't.'

March could see that her last remark had definitely hit home, May heaving a deep sigh.

And she meant it about the farm. She wanted to keep it—certainly didn't want to sell it to someone like Jude Marshall!—but she wasn't about to insist on keeping the farm at the cost of her sister's happiness. May had already sacrificed so much for January and herself, she deserved to have some success of her own.

'January is twenty-five, and engaged to be married,' she encouraged as May still hesitated. 'I'm twenty-six, and more than capable of taking care of myself; when are you going to stop behaving like a mother hen, May?' she teased affectionately.

Her sister gave a rueful shrug. 'Probably when you find someone else to take that place in your life.'

A husband, for instance…

'That isn't going to be for years yet,' she dismissed airily. 'I may even end up that old maid Jude Marshall assumed that we all were before Max put him straight!'

'Not you, March,' May assured her laughingly. 'Underneath that gruff exterior you're the most soft-hearted of all of us. You'll marry one day, and have a houseful of children,' she added with certainty.

But it wouldn't be this house, March began to accept sadly as May cleaned and bandaged her cut finger. If May succeeded in securing the offered film role, then the farm would be sold.

It would be a sad day for all of them if that happened, but maybe that was the way it was meant to be. January would be free to enjoy her happiness as Max's wife, without any feelings of guilt because of leaving her sisters to run the farm alone; May, she was sure, was going to achieve international success an actress. And she—

Well, she had no idea what she was going to do if or when that happened, but she would do something. The job at the estate agency had only ever been a stop-gap situation, a way of bringing money into the household. Without that driving necessity, she could perhaps be a little more choosy about what she did, could maybe even find a job in an art gallery somewhere. Now that was something she would enjoy doing. She might not have sufficient talent to succeed in that field herself, but she would love to be there when other people did.

'Or maybe you'll pick up your paintbrush again,' May probed gently.

March frowned. She hadn't spoken out loud that time, she was sure, and yet the astute May had still managed to discern at least some of her thoughts.

She gave a firm shake of her head. 'I'm not good enough; we both know that.'

'I know nothing of the kind, March Calendar,' May came back impatiently. 'One art exhibition, in what was only a little local gallery anyway—'

'The owner of that "little local gallery" was the only one who would agree to show my work!'

'—does not mean you aren't good enough,' May finished determinedly.

She grimaced. 'I sold a grand total of two paintings, May,' she reminded dryly. 'And I probably only sold those two because they fitted in with the colour-scheme of the sitting-room or the loo!'

That week, two years ago, of the one and only exhibition of her work, had been the most humiliating experience of her life, mooching about the gallery day after day—much to the owner's chagrin—in the hope that someone would actually say something learned about her work!

A couple of those days only one or two people had strolled in—and that, March was convinced, had been only because they'd wanted to be somewhere dry out of the rain! A middle-aged couple on holiday from Somerset had finally bought two of the smaller paintings, but other than that the whole experience had been a waste of time.

It had certainly been humiliating enough for March never to even contemplate doing such a thing again. In fact, she had packed all her things away in the attic of the studio, and never picked up a paintbrush again...

She never would, either!

'As I remember it, May, we weren't actually discussing me,' she reminded pointedly. 'So stop trying to change the subject! Right now you are going to telephone this director. And tomorrow you are going to get on a train to London—'

'We really don't have the money for that, March.' May frowned worriedly.

'We have our emergency fund for a rainy day,' she insisted firmly. 'In my book, this counts as an emergency.'

The three sisters had several hundred pounds, left to them by their father, put away in a bank account for that 'rainy day'. January certainly wasn't going to need it, and if the farm were to be sold...

'Okay?' she prompted May forcefully.

'Okay,' May conceded dryly. 'But do give some thought to—'

'No,' she cut in decisively. 'Now go and make that telephone call so that we can get over to Aunt Lyn's.'

She breathed a sigh of relief when May did exactly

that. She hadn't thought, or talked, about her painting for a very long time, and she had no intention of doing it over the weekend, either.

That time would be spent working on the farm—and putting sight and thought of Will Davenport as far to the back of her mind as she possibly could!

Not that the former turned out to be all that difficult to do over the next two days. Because she didn't have so much as a glimpse of Will during that time!

His car was missing from the garage from early morning until early evening, and even then it was only the lights on in the studio that told of his presence there.

Leading to only one conclusion: Will Davenport was avoiding her as much as she was avoiding him!

Well, it was what she had wanted, wasn't it? Was the reason she had been so rude to him on Friday evening?

If it was what she wanted, then why did she feel so miserable…?

Why did he feel so damned miserable?

Giving March a cooling off period was the best thing to do, Will had decided after Friday evening. Stay out of her way. Give her time to get over whatever had upset her.

Which was exactly what he had done the last two days…

And in the process, he seemed to have made himself thoroughly miserable, he acknowledged ruefully as he stood at the studio window looking wistfully across at the farmhouse, the light on in the kitchen telling him exactly where March was.

May had been noticeably absent about the farm the last two days, hopefully on her trip to London, so wasn't around to invite her lonely lodger in for a cup of tea.

And he had long ago decided that inviting himself over was out of the question—if March was still in the same frame of mind as Friday evening then she was more likely to throw the tea at him than pour it into a cup! Going over and asking to borrow a cup of sugar had already been used—

The dish March had baked the apple pie in!

He had eaten the last of the pie for his lunch, the dish now washed and ready to be returned. He could stroll over and give that back to March without seeming too obvious—

Obvious about what…?

About wanting to see her. About wanting to talk to her. About just being with her.

March Calendar, he had realized this last two days of not seeing her, had very definitely got under his skin. Quite to what degree he wasn't prepared to acknowledge even to himself, he just knew that he hadn't been able to work or sleep since being at the receiving end of the sharpness of her tongue on Friday evening.

But the dish was at least a legitimate reason for him to go and knock on the kitchen door. If she took the dish and then slammed the door in his face, he would at least have tried to breach this puzzling rift that seemed to have developed between them.

Although he wasn't sure for how long…

Graham had telephoned him from London yesterday. Even admitting to March that he had sent her paintings to the other man was sure to bring about her wrath, telling her what Graham had said could prove life-threatening—to him, not Graham!

This was ridiculous, he told himself a few minutes later as he stood nervously on the doorstep after knocking on the kitchen door to the farmhouse. He was behaving like a nervous schoolboy summoned to see the headmistress, but not sure if it was for praise or punishment!

Once again he marvelled at Max for having dared to breach the Calendar bastions. Not only that, for succeeding!

The kitchen door opened with a cautious creak, March peering round the three- or four-inch opening, frowning in recognition as she saw who stood there. 'Yes?' She frowned unwelcomingly.

'You need some oil on those door hinges,' he came back lightly.

Her frown deepened irritably. 'I'll see to it later.'

'I could do it now for you if you have some—'

'Will, I'm rather busy at the moment, so if you could just say what you're doing here…?' she cut in impatiently.

'You are?' he mused; she didn't look very busy to him. In fact, from the towel she had draped about the darkness of her hair, she seemed to have just finished washing her hair.

'I am,' she confirmed shortly. 'So, if you wouldn't mind…'

'I brought your dish back.' He held it up into the thin shaft of light allowed to shine through that small door opening.

March looked at the dish, then up at Will, and then back frustratedly to the dish, as if undecided about what to do next.

Will eyed her quizzically; an uncertain March Calendar was certainly a novelty! 'Is there a problem?' he prompted sharply.

Maybe she wasn't alone? Maybe there was a man in

there with her? There was no strange car parked outside, but that didn't mean March was alone, did it?

His hands tightened about the glass dish, his mouth thinning with displeasure, gaze narrowing warily as he inwardly acknowledged just how much he disliked the idea of any other man being within ten feet of March.

'As I said, I'm busy—'

'What about the dish?' he reminded hurriedly as she would have shut the door.

March glared at him frustratedly. 'Oh, okay,' she finally sighed in capitulation, seeming to have come to some sort of decision as she allowed the door to open fully, at the same time stepping back to allow Will to come inside.

His wariness increased as he stepped inside, quickly looking about the room, some of his tension relaxing as he saw that March was alone, after all. Then why—

His mouth twitched with humour, his eyes gleaming with that suppressed laughter as, having turned to look at March, he saw the obvious reason for her previous discomfort.

She had obviously just had a bath and washed her hair, the latter wrapped in the towel, her only clothing appearing to be a cream bathrobe—something guaranteed to raise his blood pressure!

But at the moment it was definitely humour that was winning out in the emotion stakes; following her bath and washing her hair, March seemed to be in the process of paintings her nails. All of them.

She held her hands out in front of her, obviously allowing the peach lacquer on her medium-length nails to dry. Revealing the reason she had been reluctant to take the dish from him!

But it was the lacquer on her toenails that was the

cause of his amusement, wads of cotton wool between her toes allowing it to dry unsmudged. At least, he presumed that was the reason for it...

'And to think I never knew what I was missing by not having a sister,' he remarked conversationally as he put the glass dish down on one of the worktops, at the same time biting his inner lip to stop himself from laughing openly.

March glared at him, moving awkwardly across the room to sit down on one of the chairs, her heels down, her toes raised off the ground. 'Very funny!' She frowned. 'I was bored, okay,' she added defensively. 'May has been away all weekend and will continue to be away until tomorrow morning. All the work is done on the farm for this evening. As usual, there's nothing on the television—'

'So you decided to paint your toenails,' Will finished appreciatively.

'Yes!' She glared at him challengingly.

'Very sensible.' He nodded, brows raised innocently.

March looked totally unconvinced by his placating attitude. 'I've never painted my toenails before,' she defended irritably. 'It just seemed like a good thing to do at the time.' She grimaced.

Will looked down at the newly painted nails; March even had pretty feet, he realized self-derisively, long and slender, perfectly formed. As for what it was doing to his heartbeat, having March sitting feet away from him dressed only in a bathrobe...!

'Very nice,' he finally murmured gruffly, his gaze returning determinedly to her face.

March looked at him with narrowed eyes, her mouth starting to twitch, those eyes glinting with sudden humour, a humour that obviously won out as she began to chuckle self-derisively. 'I have never felt so ridiculous in my life,' she admitted with a rueful shake of her head.

He grinned. 'You haven't?'

'No,' she sighed. 'Hard as that probably is for you to believe,' she added dryly.

Will felt encouraged enough by her show of humour to sit down at the kitchen table opposite her. 'What's the verdict?' He inclined his head in the direction of her feet.

'Also ridiculous,' she came back disgustedly. 'I look like some sort of pampered princess in a harem!'

Will felt a lurch in the region of his chest at the image that thought created; he wouldn't mind having a harem of one! As long as that one was March...

'I would take it off again—' March hurried into speech as she seemed to realize she had been less than circumspect '—but the varnish remover would just ruin the nails on my hand then so that I would have to start again, and—'

'I could do it for you, if you would like me to,' Will put in lightly, at the same time hoping his eagerness to touch any part of her wasn't too obvious.

March looked across at him uncertainly, colour slowly entering her cheeks. 'No, I—I think I'll just go upstairs and put some clothes and shoes on; that will solve the problem just as well,' she said haltingly.

'Pity,' he murmured under his breath regretfully.

'Sorry?'

'Nothing.' He shook his head, smiling across at her.

She stood up abruptly. 'Er—make yourself some coffee while I'm gone, if you would like,' she told him dismissively. 'I won't be long.'

She hurried from the room.

As if the devil himself were at her heels...!

Will frowned to himself as he stood up to prepare a pot of coffee, knowing from previous visits exactly where everything was kept.

Was it the other evening that had been bothering March the last few days? Had the depth of passion they had both so obviously felt somehow frightened her?

It had frightened him too—although probably not in the way it had March!

He was thirty-seven years old, had been involved in several intimate relationships over the last fifteen or so years, but none of those women had brought out the protective instinct in him in the way that March did.

It was the weirdest emotion he had ever experienced, wanting to look after her, make sure no one hurt her, at the same time that he wanted to make love to her until she cried out for mercy!

If March felt even a tenth of that confusion, perhaps she had been right to be so cool with him on Friday evening!

Although his own confusion hadn't stopped him from coming up with any excuse this evening so that he could come over to the farmhouse to see her...

'Oh, good, you made the coffee.' March bounced cheerfully into the kitchen ten minutes later, seeming to have got over appearing to be disturbed earlier, her hair dry and gleaming darkly down her back, wearing a white tee shirt and fitted denims, her feet—and presumably those painted toenails!—hidden in a pair of green leather ankle boots. 'Not much of an improvement?' she prompted teasingly as she saw Will's gaze linger on the latter.

He gave a shake of his head. 'I've just never seen green boots before.'

'They had a red or blue pair in the shop too, but I

opted for the green,' she told him laughingly, taking over the job of pouring the coffee into two mugs. 'Do you know, you're the first person I've spoken to since May left yesterday morning?' she continued conversationally. 'I've never been here completely on my own before. I had never realized just how remote we are up in the hills here,' she added wistfully. 'In fact, the only comforting fact has been the knowledge that you were over in the studio in the evenings.' She gave him a smile as she brought their mugs of coffee over to the table.

Will grinned. 'Nice to know I'm useful for something!' At least he now knew the reason he had been invited in at all!

She gave a grimace as she sat down. 'I'm trying—not very successfully, I'll admit!—to apologize for my behaviour the last few days.' She shook her head. 'I was very rude to you on Friday evening,' she added huskily, 'and, to be honest, I've been avoiding you ever since,' she admitted quietly, nose suddenly buried in her mug of coffee.

March's honesty was something else that totally threw him, Will acknowledged a little breathlessly, wondering if he ought to own up to the same behaviour. But deciding against it. That would involve an explanation of some sort on his part, and right now he didn't really have one.

'May explained it was something she said,' he dismissed, eager to put that unpleasantness behind them now and move on. Quite where, he still had no idea, but he certainly didn't like feeling at odds with March.

'Did she?' March frowned now. 'Did she say what it was?' she added with a casualness that wasn't fooling anyone.

'No. And I didn't ask,' Will instantly reassured her.

'Have you heard from her? Are things going well for her this weekend?'

March relaxed back in her chair, a smile playing about her lips, obviously happier now that they were talking about her sister and not her own puzzling behaviour on Friday evening. 'Yes, I've heard from her. And she's going out to dinner with the director this evening. But you know May,' she added affectionately. 'She's convinced he's only taking her out in order to let her down gently.'

'That sounds like May,' he acknowledged with a chuckle.

March gave him a quizzical look. 'You like May, don't you?'

'I like all of you,' he corrected firmly. 'Even January—and I've never met her! But Max has been a good friend for over twenty years, so any woman he loves and wants to marry has to be okay with me.' Besides, if January were anything like the other two Calendar sisters, then he couldn't help but envy Max his good fortune!

She nodded. 'How do you think Jude Marshall is going to react to Max's resignation?'

Will gave the matter some thought. Jude was a shrewd businessman, and a very successful one, but the three men had been friends since school-days...

'I don't think Jude will let a little thing like Max's choice of wife influence his complete confidence in him as his lawyer,' he answered truthfully. 'I don't think he will accept Max's resignation,' he explained as March looked puzzled.

'You don't?' She looked astounded now.

'Jude isn't the monster you think him, you know,' Will told her with a smile, knowing even as the words left his mouth that he had once again said the wrong thing, March instantly bristling with resentment, her eyes sparkling challengingly.

'You're bound to say that, aren't you?' she scorned dismissively. 'After all, you're just another friend of his!'

Damn, this was hard work! Like walking through a minefield without any indications of where the explosions might be or when they might occur!

Was it really worth it?

Hell, yes!

If being with March was less than relaxing, it was certainly better than not being with her at all; the last couple of days had been some of the most boring he had ever spent, even his work not having held his interest in the way that it usually did as thoughts of March had gone round and round in his head. All without any conclusions or answers as to why he felt the way he did...

'Maybe it would be better if we didn't discuss Jude,' he began frowningly.

'Have you spoken to him recently?' March came back scathingly.

As a matter of fact, he had spoken to the other man the previous day. But he didn't think telling March now of Jude's intended visit to England was going to please her.

The opposite, he would have thought!

Just as telling her about the paintings he had sent to Graham in London wasn't going to please her!

No, he decided, both those things could wait until May returned tomorrow. May had a soothing influence on March—and if that failed, she could always stand between them when March tried to strangle him!

CHAPTER TEN

MARCH watched Will as a number of emotions flashed across his handsome features, caution finally seeming to win out as a shutter came down over those sky-blue eyes.

What was he keeping from her? she wondered. What *wasn't* he keeping from her? followed quickly on its heels!

She had felt extremely foolish when Will had arrived earlier, but hoped that she had slightly redeemed herself during the last few minutes, apology for her behaviour Friday evening included. Talking of Jude Marshall was guaranteed to put them back where they had begun half an hour ago!

'Sorry.' She held up an apologetic hand. 'I shouldn't have asked you that. It's none of my business whether or not you've spoken to—' 'that man' didn't exactly sound conciliatory, did it? '—to Jude Marshall,' she concluded evenly. 'More coffee?' she offered lightly as she saw his mug was empty, standing to pick up the two mugs.

'No.' Will stood up too.

'No?' she echoed huskily, the atmosphere in the kitchen suddenly so charged—with something!—that she could almost taste it.

'No,' he repeated softly, reaching out to take the two mugs from her unresisting hands to place them back on the table. 'March, you are without doubt the most puzzling woman—'

121

'You've already told me that,' she put in quickly.

'The fact that I'm repeating it must mean it's true!' He gave an impatient shake of his head. 'March, a few minutes ago you were spoiling for yet another fight, and yet now you're offering me more coffee...' He gave a dazed shake of his head.

She gave the wince of a smile. 'A little too change-able, would you say?' she acknowledged self-derisively.

'I would say, yes,' he confirmed frustratedly.

March gave a heavy sigh. 'I don't want to fight with you, Will. I just want—'

'Yes?' he prompted tautly as she broke off abruptly.

She didn't know what she wanted! All that she did know with any certainty was that the last two days had been completely miserable, partly because May was away and she was on her own, but also because she was very aware of the strain between herself and Will.

Also the reason for it...

Could May possibly be right? Could she already be in love with this man? If the erratic beat of her heart, the dampness of the palms of her hands, the almost weak-kneed feeling she had whenever she looked at him were anything to go by, then the answer was yes!

And if that truly were the case, then what was she going to do about it?

Uncertainty of any kind didn't come naturally to March; she had always been totally decisive, and quick to act on those decisions. But looking at Will, acknowl-edging that breathless, weak-kneed feeling, she had no idea what she was going to do about her love for him!

'I don't know what I want,' she finally answered hus-kily, dark lashes fanning down over her cheeks as she looked down at her feet.

But she heard Will move, felt his hands warm on her

upper arms as he shook her slightly. 'March, look at me,' he instructed softly, his gaze questioning as she raised her lashes. 'Do you want me?'

She gasped her surprise at the question. 'Now who's being excessively blunt?' she came back incredulously.

He gave a self-derisive grimace. 'Maybe I've decided to meet fire with fire!'

Just the mention of that word was enough to bring back memories of her time in his arms on Thursday evening, when the fire of their desire had threatened to totally engulf her.

'At least answer me, March.' He shook her gently.

She moistened suddenly dry lips, swallowing hard, knowing her panic must be evident on her face as she sought to find an answer that wouldn't sweep them both away in that torrent of passion, a passion she simply had no defences against.

Will gave a choked noise in his throat, his hands moving to sweep her into his arms, holding her tightly against his chest as he stroked the silky softness of her hair. 'I didn't mean right this minute, silly,' he soothed huskily.

Her cheek lay against his jumper-covered shoulder, the rapid beat of his heart clearly discernible to her. 'It's just for future reference?' she teased.

'Something like that,' he agreed, the sound of laughter in his voice.

Not laughter at her but with her, March easily read. Just as she knew this situation was fast becoming dangerous. They were completely alone here, would continue to be so until May returned some time tomorrow. And even if she did want him, as he appeared to want her, they didn't know each other well enough to—

'Tell you what, March.' Will moved back with a suddenness that startled her, once again holding her at arm's length as he looked down at her with warm blue eyes. 'Let's go out somewhere and have a drink. Apart from a couple of lunches we haven't actually been out together,' he added persuasively.

It was almost as if he could read her thoughts, as if he knew of her reluctance to admit her attraction to him when they were alone here like this.

And maybe he did know, she acknowledged ruefully; her face was like glass, revealed every emotion that she thought or felt.

'It seems a pity to waste your freshly painted nails,' Will added teasingly as she still hesitated. 'All of them!'

She gave him a rueful smile. 'I'm never going to live that down, am I?'

He grinned. 'Not in this lifetime, no.'

'Okay,' she accepted abruptly, not wanting to dwell on that 'lifetime' comment. 'There's a nice old-fashioned pub a couple of miles from here, we could go there.'

Will nodded, watching her as she collected her coat from the back of the door. 'I think I had lunch there the other day. I don't like to cook, okay,' he defended as she gave him a scornful look.

'Okay,' she acknowledged dryly. 'Your car or mine?' she added mockingly.

'Definitely mine!' He gave a shake of his head. 'I doubt I would fit into yours, anyway.'

March doubted he would either. Quite tall herself, her own head only just missed touching the roof of her little car; Will would simply end up with a crick in his neck.

Besides, it was certainly an experience to be a passenger in the Ferrari, to sink into the leather seat, the array of dials on the dashboard looking too confusing for her to even try to identify what they were all for.

It was also a relief to be away from the intimacy of the farmhouse. Something she was sure Will had been well aware of when he'd suggested they go out...

She studied him surreptitiously as he drove, admiring the assured economy of movement, his hands long and slender on the wheel. Artistically beautiful hands, she realized wonderingly, lean and sensitive.

'Did you always want to be an architect?' she prompted interestedly once they were seated inside the saloon bar of the tiny pub, only one other couple seated on the other side of the room on this quiet Sunday evening.

Will gave her a sharp look. 'Is this a trick question?'

'Sorry?' She frowned her puzzlement.

Will looked decidedly unhappy. 'If I answer this question honestly, are you going to get up and walk out of here?'

March eyed him warily now. Obviously he hadn't always wanted to be an architect, but what could possibly be so controversial about what he had wanted to be that he thought she might actually get up and leave once he had answered her?

Will could see that March was completely perplexed by his reluctance to answer her, knew she had no idea what he was talking about.

Maybe it was his own guilty conscience because of what he had done? Or maybe it was just a reluctance on his part to talk about anything that was going to upset or disturb March. As his truthful answer was sure to do!

Getting March to come out with him in the first place had been a miracle in itself; he didn't want her getting up and walking out on him before they had even taken a sip of the drinks he had just bought them!

'I need your promise first that you won't do that,' he prompted ruefully.

'Okay—I promise.' March shrugged dismissively.

'Too easy.' Will gave a firm shake of his head. 'I'm really serious about this, March.'

'I can see that you are,' she acknowledged slowly, her puzzlement obviously deepening. 'Is it really that bad?' she said wonderingly.

'Depends on your point of view,' he answered evasively.

'And from my point of view…?'

'It just might be.' He nodded consideringly.

'Okay.' She shrugged. 'I promise, no matter what you say your initial career choice was—manager of a nudist colony, astronaut, striptease artist—that I won't walk out of here.'

Will drew in a deep breath. 'The last was close.'

Her eyes widened incredulously. 'Striptease artist!'

He gave her a reproving frown. 'The last word,' he corrected impatiently, only vaguely aware of the interest of the couple seated across the room as their own voices rose in volume.

'The last—ah.' March became suddenly still, frozen in the act of picking up her glass of white wine and taking a sip.

'You promised you wouldn't walk out,' Will reminded evenly, at the same time giving her anxious looks.

'An artist,' she muttered huskily. 'You wanted to be an artist?' Her voice was tight with emotion, her face pale, a nerve pulsing in her tightly clenched jaw.

'I did.' He looked away, deliberately giving her time

to absorb the information. 'As it turned out, I have a little artistic flare, and I'm good at drawing straight lines. Perfect for being an architect. But not good enough to be an artist of any interest to anyone but myself,' he added flatly, his gaze returning to March's face.

She still looked pale, but her other emotions were under control now as she gave a dismissive shrug. 'It seems there are a lot of us about,' she murmured softly.

He was never going to get a more perfect opening than this, he knew that. But he was reluctant to break the guarded friendship that they had only recently built up. But not to tell March now about her paintings that he had sent to London, what Graham had to say about them, would put them back to the very beginning. And he didn't want to go there.

'You haven't tried your wine yet,' he delayed lightly, watching as she obediently took a sip.

Not that he thought her acquiescence was going to last for very long; a submissive March Calendar was totally unimaginable!

'March—'

'Will—'

They both began talking at once, both breaking off at the same time too to look at each other with rueful derision.

Will drew in another deep breath. 'I know it's ungentlemanly of me to go first—' he grimaced, his hand tightening around his glass of beer '—but I really have got to get this off my chest.'

March tilted her head to one side, looking at him quizzically. 'I think I really would have preferred it if you had wanted to be the astronaut!'

He gave the ghost of a smile in response to her obvious effort to try and lighten the conversation. 'It probably would have been easier,' he agreed ruefully. 'But "easy" isn't a word I've ever associated with being around you,' he acknowledged dryly.

March smiled too now. 'Are you complaining?'

Strangely enough, he wasn't. It was the fact that March was so prickly and outspoken that had piqued his interest in the first place. What continued to hold his interest!

He reached out and put his hand over one of hers as it rested on the table-top. 'Not at all,' he assured her warmly.

She allowed her hand to remain beneath his. 'Something you had to get off your chest?' she reminded huskily.

He closed his eyes, shutting out the beauty of her face. Maybe if he didn't look at her...

Damn it, he didn't have this much trouble dealing with people who wanted impossible things in their architectural designs, had seen grown men cry when he'd told them that their design simply wouldn't work on a practical basis!

He opened his eyes, looking determinedly into March's questioning eyes. 'Your paintings are of interest, March,' he stated evenly. 'In fact—'

'How do you know that?' she cut in suspiciously. 'You've been back up in the attic!' she added accusingly, snatching her hand away from his to clasp it together with her other hand in her lap, grey-green eyes starting to sparkle with anger as she glared at him.

'I was—curious,' he admitted, his grimace apologetic. 'And so I—'

'And so you went back up into the attic,' she finished tautly, turning on the padded bench-seat to glare at him now. 'After I expressly told you not to. How dare you—?'

'It's worse than that, I'm afraid, March,' he interrupted determinedly; he had started this, he had to finish it. 'On Friday I parcelled up half a dozen of what I thought were the best ones and sent them to a friend of mine in London who runs a gallery—'

'You did what?' she bit out forcefully, her cheeks white now, her eyes huge in that paleness.

'Graham is something of an expert,' he defended. 'Plus he's always on the lookout for new talent—'

'How dare you?' she burst out furiously. 'How *dare* you?' she repeated incredulously.

'March, just listen to me—'

'No,' she rasped uncompromisingly. 'Absolutely not,' she snapped, standing up to fling her shoulder bag over her arm.

'You promised you wouldn't get up and leave,' he reminded her with a pained wince.

She glared down at him. 'That was over your initial choice of career,' she ground out harshly. 'This is something else entirely.'

He could see that it was. Could see that in March's eyes he really had gone too far.

But what else could he have done? He had looked at the paintings, believed they were good, but at the same time known that if he'd asked March first she would never have agreed to sending any of them off to Graham.

But did that make it right for him to go behind her back and send the paintings to Graham without her knowledge?

Obviously, in March's eyes, the answer to that was a definite no!

'Don't you want to know what Graham had to say about them?' he cajoled reasonably.

Her eyes flashed sparks of green. 'No, I do not! You are without doubt the most interfering, self-satisfied, arrogant individual it has ever been my misfortune to meet! And, in future, I would suggest you stay well out of my way,' she added forcefully. 'As for the paintings—get them back,' she told him furiously. 'Or risk answering to the police for being in possession of stolen property—'

'But I'm not in possession—Graham is.' He knew it was the wrong thing to say as soon as he had said it. This was absolutely no time for levity.

No time at all, he discovered a few seconds later as March poured the contents—the almost-full contents!—of her glass over the top of his head!

She slammed the empty glass down on the table-top with such force it was surprising it didn't shatter from the impact. 'You have twenty-four hours to get those paintings back,' she warned him fiercely. 'After that, I shall put the whole thing in the hands of the police. I mean it, Will,' she added harshly.

Through the wine dripping down from his hair he could see that she did. He could also see that she had never looked more beautiful, her cheeks flushed, her eyes glowing fiercely, every inch of her slender body tense with anger.

But it was because he did have wine dripping down his face that he knew it wasn't a good time for him to make such an observation—she might pick up his own glass of beer next and throw that over him, too!

'Do you believe me?' she prompted tautly.

He nodded. 'In the circumstances, it would be hard

not to believe you.' He sighed, licking the white wine from his lips as it dripped down his face.

'Think yourself lucky it wasn't a whole bottle!' Her eyes glowed triumphantly as she looked at him.

'Oh, I do,' he acknowledged dryly, frowning as she turned away. 'Where are you going?'

'Home,' she answered decisively without even glancing back at him.

'But—'

'I'll enjoy the walk,' she bit out dismissively. 'You stay and finish your beer.' She crossed the room in four strides of those gloriously long legs, the door closing firmly behind her seconds later.

Leaving the room suddenly extremely quiet, only the logs crackling in the fireplace to break that silence as Will became aware of the unmistakable interest of the other couple in the room.

And who could blame them? Will was sure they weren't usually treated to such a display on a quiet Sunday evening out at the pub!

He shrugged across at the elderly couple. 'I guess she would have preferred red wine rather than the white!' he murmured ruefully.

The smiles they gave him were ones of relief rather than anything else; perhaps they had thought there was a possibility of his starting to throw the furniture around now that March had left!

March...

He gave an inward grown. He had really blown it with her this evening. He had known she was going to be displeased about his having taken the paintings without her permission, but he had hoped to be able to sit down and talk to her calmly about the subject. The glass of wine tipped over his head had told him that wasn't going to be possible!

God knew what was going to happen when Graham himself turned up tomorrow!

CHAPTER ELEVEN

MARCH was cold by the time she reached the farmhouse, slightly damp from the rain that had started to fall—and extremely irritated with Will for his high-handed behaviour.

How dared he—

There was someone in the farmhouse!

She had switched off all the lights inside the farmhouse before they'd gone out. She was sure that she had.

And yet a light shone in the kitchen now. Also on the landing upstairs.

She was just in the mood to deal with burglars—not!

Where was Will when she needed him? He was all too eager to stick his nose in where it wasn't wanted, and now that he was needed he was probably still at the pub calmly drinking his beer! He certainly hadn't passed her in the car as she'd walked the couple of miles back home.

She moved stealthily over to the kitchen window, peering inside, careful not to show too much of her face, in case the burglars should be looking her way. The kitchen was empty.

They were upstairs, then. Not that there was anything there to steal. The few pieces of jewellery the sisters had accumulated over the years were worn by them all on a day-to-day basis, and they certainly weren't of the calibre to interest a burglar!

But that didn't alter the fact that there was someone inside the farmhouse who shouldn't be there.

Or the fact that the telephone, her only means of communication, was in the hallway, where she would be heard if she attempted to telephone the police from there! What—

The mobile! They all shared a mobile-telephone for when they were out and about on the farm, and she could see it now lying on top of one of the kitchen units. If she could just—

She stiffened as she heard a noise behind her, her hand raised defensively as she turned sharply.

'Why are you looking in the kitchen window in that furtive way?' May prompted frowningly, standing back to look at March consideringly.

March swallowed—her heart, mainly! 'Why aren't *you* still in London?' she returned accusingly, May obviously having just returned from checking on the ewes.

Her sister shrugged, turning away to open the kitchen door. 'I had concluded my business there, I didn't see any reason for me to waste the money for an extra night in a London hotel.' She shrugged dismissively, her voice fading slightly as she entered the kitchen.

March followed her sister a little dazedly; May was the last person she had expected to see this evening.

'I also thought—mistakenly, as it turns out—that you might be feeling in need of a little company after being on your own all weekend,' May added with raised brows as she turned from putting the kettle on the Aga. 'But when I got back an hour ago the farm was deserted...'

March felt the warmth in her cheeks at her sister's speculative look. 'Will took me out for a drink.' There was no point in lying about it.

'Really?' May drawled speculatively. 'He doesn't appear to have brought you back again!'

March gave a pained grimace at the indisputable truth

of that statement. Will obviously hadn't returned with her; May would have heard the powerful engine of his car if that were the case.

She avoided her sister's gaze. 'No. Well—'

'March, have you been upsetting our lodger again?' her sister interrupted laughingly.

She winced, knowing she might as well come clean about what she had done; May was sure to find out eventually anyway! 'Do you think pouring white wine over the top of his head could be classed as that?'

May spluttered with the laughter she could no longer contain. 'I think,' she managed to murmur between chuckles. 'Oh, March, you have no idea how much I've missed you!' She quickly crossed the room to give March a hug. 'What did the poor man do to deserve that?' she prompted, her arm still about March as she leant against her affectionately.

'Don't ask!' she dismissed hardly. 'Just tell me what happened in London. How did the screen test go? Is this David Melton single and gorgeous? When do you—' She broke off abruptly as her sister stiffened before moving away, a shutter seeming to come down over her face, her emotions suddenly unreadable. 'May…?' she prompted uncertainly. 'I thought you were supposed to go out to dinner with the director this evening?' That had certainly been the plan when she had spoken to May earlier this morning…

'Change of plan,' her sister dismissed, her face turned away in profile. 'I'm not going to do the film, March,' she added huskily.

'You aren't?' March was stunned; May had sounded so positive and excited when the two of them had spoken on the telephone this morning. 'But you said everything had gone well. That—'

'I was wrong,' May dismissed hardly.

'But—'

'Just leave it, will you, March?' May's gaze was bleak as she turned to frown at March. 'I was a fool ever to think—' She broke off, shaking her head. 'It was a mistake, okay?' she snapped forcefully. 'A total, disastrous mistake, much worse than I imagined. And I don't ever want the subject mentioned again!' she added fiercely.

'But I don't understand,' March murmured dazedly.

May gave a humourless smile. 'There's nothing to understand. Now could we—' She broke off as the sound of a powerful engine could be heard entering the yard. 'I believe our lodger has returned,' she murmured dryly.

March was well aware of that, could feel the colour leaving her cheeks even as the engine was switched off, followed by the closing of the garage door. If Will came over here—

'Perhaps you should tell me—what did he do to get wine poured over him?' May prompted curiously.

Her mouth tightened as she recalled exactly what Will had done to merit her wrath, his arrogant high-handedness. If he had the temerity to come over here after what he had done—he would learn all over again of her displeasure!

'Never mind,' she muttered in reply, moving silently over to the kitchen window, her gaze narrowing with satisfaction as she saw Will making his way slowly up the metal steps to the studio.

No doubt so that he could have a shower and wash the white wine from his hair!

She was smiling as she turned back to face May, that smile fading to a look of innocence as her sister raised questioning brows. 'He's arrogance personified, okay,' she muttered defensively.

'Will is?' May sounded sceptical. 'He's nowhere near as arrogant as Max,' she pointed out dryly. 'Or Jude Marshall, either, for that matter,' she added hardly. 'In fact, next to the two of them, Will is a perfect pussycat!'

'That's only because you don't know him the way that I do,' March accused, still furiously angry at his having even looked at her paintings after being told not to do so, let alone dared to send them off to a friend of his in London. As for the humiliation of what his friend would have told him about them...!

Admit it, March, she sighed heavily—it was that criticism, relayed through Will, that would have been so impossible to hear. The reason she had so quickly silenced him on the subject. The reason she refused to even discuss it.

'Oh, no, you don't,' she told May firmly, turning determinedly from the window. 'We were discussing you, not Will Davenport,' she dismissed scornfully. 'Now what—'

'March, I may not show it as often as you, or even January for that matter,' May interrupted with quiet finality, 'but I can be as stubborn as the two of you when I choose to be!'

'And on the subject of the screen test and film, you choose to be,' March guessed slowly.

Her sister's mouth was tight. 'I do.'

Which didn't satisfy March one little bit. What had happened in London? Hadn't the screen test gone well? Had this director chap made a pass at May? What had happened?

May gave a rueful laugh as she watched the emotions flickering across March's face. 'Frustrating, isn't it?'

'Very,' she acknowledged heavily.

May shrugged. 'I'm sorry about that, but I really have

said the last word on the subject. Which means, if you still feel the same way, that we can consider keeping the farm, after all…' she prompted searchingly. 'But only if you still feel the same way…?'

When it was put like that, March really had no idea whether she wanted to keep the farm now or not. She had spent the last few days reconciling herself to the fact that it would have to be sold, making tentative plans for what she would do when it was. Now, it seemed, they were back to square one.

'I have no idea what I feel on the subject any more,' she answered truthfully.

'Think about it.' May reached up to give her shoulder a reassuring squeeze. 'I'm quite happy to fall in with whatever you want to do. But right now, I just want to go to bed and have a decent night's sleep.' She shook her head. 'London is so big and noisy, I haven't slept at all well since I went away.'

March sat in the kitchen drinking tea long after May had gone up to bed, totally confused as to what they should do now. If they agreed to sell the farm, without the offer of the film role, what would May do instead?

In the circumstances, it no longer seemed to make sense to sell the farm…

Which left them all precisely back where they had been several weeks ago—determined not to sell the farm, with Jude Marshall as the enemy.

And, as his latest envoy, Will Davenport definitely came under the same heading!

'For goodness' sake, Will, anyone would think you were terrified of the woman!' Graham derided ruefully.

Will glanced at his old friend from art-school days, having just driven to the railway station to pick him up. Along with March's paintings…

And Graham was wrong; he wasn't so much 'terrified' of March, as slightly apprehensive as to what she might say to the poor, unsuspecting Graham. Until the other man had been at the receiving end of March's caustic tongue he could have no idea how lethal it could be.

'I'm just warning you that she isn't at all happy about your having looked at her paintings.' Will shrugged.

'*You* sent them to me!' his friend reminded him frowningly.

He grimaced. 'Unhappy doesn't even begin to describe how she feels towards me for having done that!'

Graham laughed softly, short and slender, with warm blue eyes, his blond hair thinning at the crown. Baldness, he claimed, was like insanity—you inherited it from your children, of which he had three!

'Finally met your match, have you, Davenport?' Graham teased now. 'I knew it would happen one day,' he added with satisfaction. 'I was already looking forward to making the acquaintance of March Calendar, the artist.' He settled more comfortably into his seat. 'But now it's doubly intriguing.'

'Graham—'

'I've had to listen to your jokes about domesticity for years,' Graham continued serenely. 'It looks as if the tables are about to be turned!' He grinned unabashedly.

'You have that all wrong.' Will shook his head. 'If anything, March hates me!'

'Even better.' Graham's grin widened.

'With friends like you…' Will gave Graham a last frowning look before turning his attention back to the road.

It had been arranged between the two men for Graham

to arrive in Yorkshire around Monday tea time, Will seeing absolutely no point in his arriving during the day when March was out at work. The only problem with that was Will still hadn't told March of the other man's arrival. The *only* problem!

March had been furious enough last night, when he had only mentioned having sent those paintings to Graham, to throw a glass of wine over him; what might she do when he went to the farmhouse door this evening with Graham at his side? Oh, well, Graham couldn't say that he hadn't tried to warn him!

Although that didn't help ease Will's trepidation as he drove into the farmyard to park his car in the garage, March already at home if her little red car parked near the house was anything to go by.

But, with any luck, May would be home too by now, which should help to diffuse the situation somewhat.

'Will you stop grinning in that imbecilic manner?' he snapped at Graham as the two men got out of the car. 'You look almost ghoulish!'

The other man chuckled. 'If you could only see the look on your face—you would be laughing too!' He shook his head incredulously. 'March Calendar must be really something!'

Oh, she was 'something', all right, Will accepted heavily; stubborn, pigheaded, unreasonable, beautiful, *desirable*—

'Let's go,' he told the other man determinedly—the sooner he got this over with, the better. After all, it couldn't really be that bad, could it…?

'With pleasure,' Graham acceded happily, following behind Will's long strides towards the farmhouse.

He couldn't exactly blame Graham for this teasing attitude. Graham had married shortly after leaving art school, his three children arriving in the three years following this, and for years Will had teased him about his obvious enjoyment of his family lifestyle. As far as Graham was concerned, the tables were now turned as regards teasing!

And he was prevaricating, Will acknowledged ruefully as he stood outside the farmhouse door. If May answered his knock, the first few minutes would probably be fine, but if it were March who came to the door…!

'What do you want?' she rasped after jerking the door open, the squeak of the hinges telling Will that she still hadn't put any oil on them.

Although he realized that was the least of his problems as March glared at him with obvious dislike, also aware of Graham's continuing enjoyment of the situation as he stood slightly behind him.

'Er—is May at home?' he prompted, wincing as the sound of Graham's stifled laughter from behind him told him he had sounded like a gawky teenager come round to ask for a date!

'She is.' March nodded, at the same time making no effort to go and find her sister, just continuing to stand there looking at him with those cold grey-green eyes.

His mouth thinned at her deliberate awkwardness. 'Then could I speak to her?' he snapped his impatience.

March gave a slight inclination of her head, her gaze flicking briefly over Graham before returning coldly to Will. 'Perhaps you would care to wait while I go and ask her.' But instead of inviting them inside, March firmly closed the door in their faces.

'Very hospitable,' Graham murmured humorously as he moved to stand beside Will.

He shook his head. 'She isn't usually this— She's

annoyed with me, that's all.' He sighed heavily, knowing from March's attitude that she hadn't softened towards him at all in the intervening twenty-four hours since she had thrown that glass of wine over him.

'She's magnificent!' Graham whistled admiringly.

He turned to glare at his friend. 'I would like to wring her beautiful neck!' he ground out fiercely.

Graham grinned knowingly. 'Amongst other things!'

Was it so obvious how he felt about March? Damn it, he didn't know how he felt about March. She was infuriating, frustrating, just plain awkward most of the time. But the rest of the time he wanted to sweep her up into his arms and kiss her into submission…!

'Cheer up, Will.' Graham reached out and gave his arm a playful punch. 'Perhaps she'll feel more kindly towards you after I've had a little chat with her.'

And perhaps she wouldn't. There was simply no knowing from one minute to the next how March was going to react to something. She could just end up hating him more than ever…

If that were possible!

CHAPTER TWELVE

'YOU'VE left Will standing where—?' May gasped disbelievingly as she hurried down the stairs two at a time. 'And he had someone with him too!' She turned briefly to give March a reproving look before hurrying through to the kitchen.

March followed slowly behind her, in no mood to talk to Will, or his friend, and not too bothered at being polite about it either. After the day she had just had—!

By the time she entered the kitchen quietly a few minutes later Will and the other man had been invited in by May and were seated at the kitchen table while May put the kettle on for a drink.

'Don't be silly, Will, of course you don't have to ask our permission to have a friend stay overnight at the studio,' May dismissed laughingly as she got out the cups.

'Does March feel the same way?'

March bridled resentfully as she suddenly became the focus of attention as she stood back against the door, frowning darkly at Will before her gaze moved to the man sitting next to him. 'You would be the "friend" in question?' she prompted speculatively.

The man was short and slight, with thinning blond hair, blue eyes looking huge behind gold-framed glasses.

'Hey, I'm not that sort of "friend".' The man laughed dismissively as he held up defensive hands. 'I have a wife and three children at home,' he added for good measure.

March could feel the colour warm her cheeks, deliberately avoiding Will's impatient glare. 'And home is where, Mr—?' she prompted politely.

'London,' the slight man replied evenly. 'And the name is Whitford, Graham Whitford.'

He said the last almost as if—as if—

Graham!

Hadn't Will told her that he had sent her paintings to a friend of his called Graham, a Graham who also lived in London...?

She turned to Will sharply, eyes narrowed suspiciously, knowing by the suddenly too-innocent expression on his face as his gaze steadily met hers that her conclusions had been correct; this was the same Graham that he had sent her paintings to.

But what was the man doing here?

Never mind what he was doing here—today had already been disastrous enough; she simply couldn't deal with anything else this evening.

'If you'll excuse me, I just have to go outside for a while.' She pushed herself away from the door, looking to neither left nor right as she grabbed her coat from the hook and wrenched open the door.

'Could I come with you?' It was Graham Whitford who spoke, standing up as March turned to look at him frowningly. 'Will told me earlier that it's lambing time, and—'

'He did?' March turned to give Will a scathing look.

'He did,' Graham confirmed lightly. 'Having been born and brought up in London, my kids would be thrilled to bits if I can tell them I've seen some newborn lambs,' he added cajolingly.

Because he had sensed she was about to refuse his request, March realized ruefully. She wasn't in the mood to talk to any friend of Will's, but especially the one he had sent her paintings to!

'A lamb is a lamb.' She shrugged dismissively.

Graham grimaced. 'I'm more used to seeing them as the Sunday roast, served with mint sauce!'

March glared at him for his levity. 'You're welcome to tag along if you really want to,' she conceded ungraciously.

'I want to,' Graham assured her determinedly, moving to accompany her outside.

March shot Will a last resentful glare before venturing out into the chilling wind, leaving it up to Graham Whitford to keep up with her if that was what he chose to do.

He did, easily matching his strides to hers, despite being a couple of inches shorter than March.

'He was only trying to be helpful, you know.' Graham spoke quietly at her side.

March had been so deep in thought—angry ones, directed at Will!—that it took her several seconds to take in what the other man had just said. But once she had, her mouth tightened ominously. 'Most interfering people prefer to see their actions in that way, don't you think?' she bit out disgustedly.

She really was not in the mood for this! Today had already been awful, everything such a shambles—to have to stand here and listen to this man's learned opinion of work he should never have seen in the first place was just too much.

And then there was Graham himself, a pleasant-faced man, who really shouldn't have been put in this position, either.

He gave a shake of his head as he followed her inside the lambing shed. 'Will is the least interfering person that I know—wow,' he suddenly breathed in a hushed voice, moving past March to stand next to a pen where a ewe was happily feeding her two newly born lambs. 'Do they always do that?' He watched in fascination as the lambs' stubby tails wagged in ecstasy.

March's expression softened as she moved to stand beside him, arms resting on top of the pen, never having lost her own sense of wonder at this maternal bliss. 'They do,' she confirmed huskily. 'Life is that uncomplicated for them,' she added wistfully, overwhelmed with how complicated her own life suddenly seemed to have become.

'March, I would like to put on an exhibition of your work.' Graham Whitford's gaze didn't leave the ewe and her lambs as he spoke evenly. 'With your agreement, of course,' he added softly.

Once again he spoke with such quiet calmness that it took March several seconds to take in exactly what he had said. But once she had, the angry colour flooded her cheeks as she turned to glare at him. 'Really?' she snapped sarcastically, giving a disgusted shake of her head. 'And whose idea was that?'

He shrugged. 'Well, Will is responsible for sending me some of your work, of course, but I choose who to exhibit in my own gallery.' The last was stated as fact, not arrogance.

March gave another shake of her head. 'Will must really be a good friend of yours. Or perhaps—'

'March, I don't—'

'Or perhaps it was someone else's idea, after all…!' she finished determinedly as her earlier scepticism turned to a deeper suspicion. 'Perhaps it was another "friend" who put the idea in your head?'

Graham gave a perplexed frown. 'I have no idea—'

'I'm referring to Jude Marshall!' she burst in accusingly.

'Jude...?' Graham echoed slowly, obviously familiar with the name.

As she had known he would be! Damn Will Davenport. Damn him!

She nodded abruptly. 'You do know him, don't you?' she stated flatly.

Graham shrugged. 'I've been—acquainted with Jude, for several years, yes,' he confirmed somewhat dazedly. 'But I fail to see what he has to do with my wanting to exhibit your work in my gallery?'

'Oh, please, do stop insulting my intelligence!' March snapped disgustedly, at last knowing exactly what was going on here.

Offer her an exhibition of her work, in London no less, and yet another Calendar sister was neatly out of the way. At least, long enough for Jude Marshall to step in and buy their farm out from under their noses.

'What did he do, offer you money to exhibit my work for the few weeks it would take to distract me?' she continued heatedly, hands clenched into fists at her sides, so angry now that she wanted to hit someone. And it wasn't Graham Whitford!

'Offer me—!' Graham looked astounded at the suggestion. 'March, I can assure you—'

'Oh, don't bother!' she cut in scathingly. 'I sincerely hope that you got one of them to pay your expenses for coming all the way up here—because you have had a completely wasted journey!' She glared at him. 'You see, I know that my work is rubbish,' she scorned. 'Innocently rural rubbish!' she added for good measure, each word cutting into her like a knife.

That much had become obvious to her during that

short local exhibition—she wasn't about to further humiliate herself in the capital of the country!

'But—'

'Oh, I don't blame you,' she assured Graham Whitford heavily. 'Business is business, and all that.'

No, she knew exactly whom she blamed—and one of them was sitting across in the farmhouse with May right this minute!

She marched over to the door. 'Make sure you lock the shed once you've had your fill of the newborns,' she told Graham hardly.

'I—but where are you going?' Graham looked completely confused by the way this conversation had turned out.

'To speak to your accomplice!' Her eyes briefly glowed with her anger before she wrenched the shed door open, slamming it shut behind her as she stormed across to the farmhouse.

How dared he? How dared Will Davenport do this to her?

To offer to pay some poor little gallery owner to exhibit her work in order to get her out of the way and leave the coast clear for Jude Marshall to snap up the Calendar farm!

It was worse than despicable—it was cruel and unkind. To have Graham Whitford come here, to offer her an exhibition, to give her hope that her work might be good after all, only for the exhibition to be a flop yet again, and in London of all places.

This was by far and away the most hurtful thing Will Davenport had ever done to her!

'March refuses to talk about the reasons behind it,' May was telling Will frowningly as March burst into the room, bringing a blast of cold air in with her as she slammed the door behind her.

But that blast of cold air, Will realized as he looked warily at March, was as nothing to the cold fury that her gaze shot across the room at him!

He stood up slowly. 'What have you done with Graham…?' he said slowly, at the same time chastising himself for the heat of desire he felt as he watched her breasts quickly rise and fall in her agitation; this was most definitely not the time to feel desire for March Calendar!

'Figuratively or literally?' March spat back forcefully.

'March—'

'I should stay out of this if I were you, May.' Will spoke gently to the elder sister as she appealed to March, his narrowed gaze remaining fixed on the younger sister. An obviously furious March. 'Both,' he answered March abruptly.

Her mouth twisted into a humourless smile. 'Literally I've left him looking at the lambs. Figuratively I've left him under no illusions as to what I think of him and his offer to exhibit my work. As for you—!' She crossed the room in two angry strides, her arm moving up in an arc as she gave his face a resounding slap. 'You're despicable! Absolutely and utterly beneath contempt!' Her voice shook emotionally.

'March!' May gasped her shock at her behaviour.

Will's gaze remained locked on March's, his left cheek stinging painfully from her slap, his own gaze ice cold now as he met her heated one.

A few seconds ago, as May had explained what had happened to March earlier today, he had been concerned and worried for her, but had hoped that what Graham had to tell her might help alleviate some of her worry. It seemed to have done the opposite!

'I don't think so,' he ground out as she raised her arm a second time, easily capturing her hand in one of his, crushing her fingers as his grip tightened.

'You're hurting me,' she managed to gasp accusingly.

He was hurting *her*! What the hell did she think she was doing to him? And he didn't just mean that slap, either!

His hand remained clenched around hers, feeling the fragility of her bones beneath his, but too angry himself at this moment to care. 'What the hell is wrong with you?' he demanded exasperatedly. 'Didn't Graham explain about wanting to exhibit your work—?'

'Oh, he ''explained'',' she snapped furiously, her eyes flashing with renewed anger. 'And I told him what he could do with his offer!'

The angry tension faded from Will's body as he slowly released her hand, utterly perplexed now. 'You told him—'

'What he could do with it,' March repeated scornfully, her crushed hand now cradled in her other one. 'Do you think I'm completely stupid, Will?' she challenged.

'Not completely, no,' he answered slowly, at a complete loss to know what he thought any more.

He had thought, once March got over her annoyance with him for having sent some of her paintings to Graham in the first place, that she would be over the moon about Graham's proposed exhibition of her work. Far from being over the moon, March was more angry than ever. He didn't understand her response. Any more than he understood March herself, he acknowledged heavily.

'I'm not even a little bit stupid where you're con-

cerned, Will Davenport,' March told him scathingly.
'But you can go back to Jude Marshall and tell him that
none of his schemes to get us out of here have succeeded—'

'Jude…?' Now Will really was puzzled. Puzzled? He
was more confused than he ever had been in his life
before!

'Tell him that the two remaining Calendar sisters are
staying put,' she finished hardly, looking at him challengingly.

Will shook his head, this whole conversation a complete enigma to him. But he felt too emotionally battered
at this moment to try and unravel it.

He turned to May, a May who looked even more be-
wildered by this situation than he felt. 'I'm really sorry
about this, but I think, in the circumstances, that it might
be for the best if I leave,' he told her huskily.

'Yes—go,' March agreed scathingly.

'I meant that I leave altogether.' Will still spoke to
May, too angry himself now to even look at March.
'Move out of the studio. I'm sorry,' he apologized again
as May looked stunned by the way this conversation had
turned out.

And maybe it was a little drastic for him to move out.
But at this moment—and for some time to come, he
felt—the further he was from March, the better it would
be for all of them.

Away from her—well away from her!—he might be
able to think straight, for one thing…

'I'm the one that's sorry, Will,' May assured him
softly, at the same time shooting March searching
glances, glances that obviously yielded her no answers
either. 'But maybe it would be for the best…' she allowed with a rueful shake of her head.

'Yes—go,' March looked at him scornfully. 'Run away!'

Will gave a weary sigh. 'I'm not running away, March, simply removing my obviously unwanted presence.'

She nodded scornfully. 'And take your friend with you.'

Will shrugged. 'After what you said earlier, I doubt he has any more reason to stay here than I do.'

She gave a humourless laugh. 'Well, at last we're all in agreement on something!' she scorned.

But there was something in her voice this time, a catch of emotion that made Will look at her sharply. Was that tears he could see in those beautiful defiant grey-green eyes? And if so, were they tears of anger or distress? As he could see no reason for March to feel the latter, he could only assume—

'I was a fool ever to think you might be different, Will Davenport.' She shook her head as she looked at him, the tears shimmering on her lashes now. 'A stupid, stupid fool,' she added self-disgustedly before turning on her heel and running from the room.

He could hear the sound of her feet moving rapidly up the stairs, followed seconds later by the closing of a bedroom door.

The silence she left behind her in the kitchen was filled with a tension so intense that even the clock could be heard ticking.

May's breath left her in a shaky sigh. 'Whew,' she murmured ruefully. 'I'm so sorry, Will.' She looked across at him appealingly. 'If it's any consolation, I don't think all of that anger was caused by you,' she added with a grimace.

He gave a slow shake of his head. 'It isn't,' he stated flatly.

May looked upset by his answer. 'She's just very upset about losing her job earlier,' she explained pleadingly. 'I was telling you before that I don't even know what really happened there; March just arrived home shortly after lunch to say that Clive Carter had paid her a month's salary and told her to leave.'

Will knew all that, had been as concerned earlier as May obviously was as they'd talked while March and Graham had been checking on the lambs. Especially as Will could probably guess at least some of the reason Clive Carter had dismissed March so arbitrarily—he hadn't forgotten that conversation he had had over lunch with March last week about the buying of property under its market value and then selling it on at a later date for a large profit. Either March had confronted Clive Carter with what she knew, or the man had found out that she knew. But, either way, Carter had decided to remove the problem by dismissing March.

But all of that was really irrelevant now. There was nothing Will could do to help—more to the point, nothing March would want him to do that might help. She had made it more than obvious a few minutes ago that she didn't consider anything he did to be in the least helpful.

He shook his head. 'I'm really sorry about this, May, but I—' He broke off as Graham came into the kitchen. 'How were the lambs?' he prompted his friend ruefully—goodness knew what March had said to him while they'd been outside together!

Graham had initially viewed March's work as a favour to him, although after looking at them it had obviously been Graham's own decision to offer March the showing in his gallery. From the little March had told him, his friend had had his offer very firmly thrown back in his face. Graham must be wondering what on earth he had walked into the middle of!

Graham gave a quizzical smile. 'Puzzling.'

Will nodded, grimacing. 'I thought they might have been!'

'But very interesting,' Graham added lightly as he came further into the room.

'That's one way of putting it,' Will acknowledged heavily, wishing he had never seen March's paintings, let alone involved Graham.

'Hmm.' Graham nodded consideringly. 'Would anyone care to explain to me why it is that March thinks I'm offering to exhibit her paintings because Jude Marshall is paying me to do so?' He looked first at Will, and then at May, obviously hoping that one of them would be able to enlighten him.

Oh, he could enlighten Graham, all right, Will acknowledged with rising fury as all of March's obscure references just now suddenly made complete sense.

That little—!

How dared she?

Did she really think that he had conspired—that he would have been part of some plan to—? No, not *part* of it, the *instigator* of it!

Damn it, March had gone too far this time.

Way too far!

CHAPTER THIRTEEN

'GO AWAY, May, please,' March groaned as her bedroom door opened, lying down on the bed, her face buried in the pillow. 'I really don't want to talk about this just yet,' she added emotionally.

'You may not want to talk about this,' Will Davenport was the one to answer her forcefully, standing by the bed glaring down at her in obvious fury as March spun quickly over to look up at him with wide, disbelieving eyes. 'But I certainly do!' he added grimly, his eyes a pale wintry blue.

March hastily rubbed away the tears from her cheeks, sitting up to look at him. 'And you're used to getting your own way, aren't you?' she said dully. 'You and Jude Marshall.'

His face darkened ominously. 'Let's get one thing straight, March,' he ground out furiously. 'Jude Marshall is not the monster you've built him up to be in your mind. And neither am I,' he added grimly.

Her eyes widened at this last statement. Will wasn't a monster to her, many other things, but never that.

She had looked at him downstairs a few minutes ago, the marks of her fingers still livid on the hardness of his cheek, and known that she loved him. Irrefutably. Irretrievably. Irrevocably!

And to know that she loved him in spite of everything, to know that there was no future for them, was breaking her heart into a thousand pieces.

'I—'

'I haven't finished yet, March,' Will told her harshly, his eyes glittering angrily. 'You're very fond of having your say.' His mouth twisted derisively. 'Now it's my turn.'

She swallowed hard. 'Okay.'

He gave a pained grimace. 'A quiet, acquiescent March Calendar—amazing! I suppose that it's too much to hope that it might last…?'

She gave a shrug. 'Probably,' she conceded heavily.

He gave a humourless smile. '"She was poor but she was honest." That was just one of those meaningless quotes, March,' he added disgustedly as her eyes flashed resentfully. 'Does everything have to be a minefield with you, March?' he added wearily. 'Every word weighed and measured before spoken in case it causes you insult?'

Was that really how it was when talking to her? March wondered frowningly. Had she become so prickly, so defensive, that everyone had to be careful what they said around her? Or was it only Will who felt that way…?

'Never mind.' He gave an impatient shake of his head. 'I'm well aware that nothing I do or say in the next few minutes is going to make the slightest difference to your opinion of me—'

'Then why bother to say it?' she put in softly.

'Because it will make me feel better!' Will answered her forcefully, beginning to pace up and down the bedroom. 'May told me what happened to you at work today—'

'She had no right!' March flared; the fewer people who knew what had happened at the estate agency today, the better!

'She had every right, damn it!' Will turned on her angrily. 'She's your sister; she's worried about you.'

March shook her head. 'There's no need. I'll get another job, and then—'

'Now who's running away, March?' Will challenged grimly. 'You and I both know you can't just leave that situation as it is. From what you told me, Carter is obviously breaking the law. Are you really intending to just walk away and let him get away with that?'

If it was only Clive that was involved, then the answer to that would be a definite no, but there was Michelle to consider too... Quiet, sweet Michelle, who had always been kind to her.

March's chin rose determinedly. 'I have no proof of my suspicions. Clive found the file I had been keeping locked away in my desk drawer. He's probably destroyed it by now,' she added heavily.

For months she had been troubled by the fact that properties had been sold by the agency, to what appeared to be some sort of holding company, only to reappear on the market several months later to be sold for a considerable profit.

Oh, she knew the property market was booming at the moment, but even so it had happened too often, once a month on her estimation, for it to all seem like a coincidence. Clive's response to the file she had started to keep only confirmed that opinion.

'You must have enough information stored inside your head to go to the police with your suspicions,' Will said sceptically.

Yes, she did, probably more than enough. But there was still Michelle to consider...

Will gave a disgusted shake of his head. 'Obviously I can't force you to do anything about that situation,' he rasped. 'Although I never thought of you as a coward before,' he added derisively.

Two spots of angry colour appeared in March's cheeks as she glared at him. He had no idea what he was talking about, none whatsoever.

'Life's full of surprises, isn't it?' she dismissed scathingly.

Will drew in an angry breath. 'Well, here's another one for you! Graham Whitford owns the Graford Gallery in London—mean anything to you?' he challenged impatiently.

Her eyes widened. Of course it meant something to her. The Graford Gallery was one of the most prestigious privately owned galleries in London, was patronized by art collectors from all over the world, was the leading gallery for discovering new and collectable artists—

And Graham Whitford, the owner of that gallery, had just offered her an exhibition of her work…!

'I can see that it does.' Will nodded with satisfaction, his gaze impatient. 'Do you really think a man of that calibre would risk the reputation of his gallery to exhibit an unknown artist with no talent?'

When he put it like that—!

'Worse,' Will grated harshly, 'do you think a man of that calibre would accept *money* as an inducement to risk the reputation of not only his gallery but himself as well by exhibiting that artist with no talent?'

March gave a pained wince as the full import of his words hit her like the slap in the face she had given him earlier.

Graham Whitford had really been serious about that offer of an exhibition of her work!

She swallowed hard, her hand shaking as she pushed the dark swathe of her hair back from the paleness of her cheeks. 'Maybe I was wrong about that—'

'Maybe?' Will ground out harshly.

March moistened dry lips. 'I—I—'

'Maybe you were wrong about a lot of things, March,' Will continued remorselessly over her halting reply. 'Me, in particular. You know, I came to the area knowing I wasn't exactly going to be the flavour of the month. It happens.' He shrugged. 'For different reasons, people resist change—'

'You—'

'For different reasons, they resist change,' he repeated hardly, his expression grim. 'And very often those reasons are perfectly valid—'

'As mine are,' she cut in determinedly.

'Maybe,' he conceded. 'But was that any reason for you to make my life a misery? To be rude and obstructive at every turn? To suspect my every motive?'

'You work for Jude Marshall!' she reminded accusingly.

'At this moment in time, yes, I do.' He nodded tersely. 'But I offered to work with you on this,' he reminded coldly. 'I suggested days ago that there must be some way you and I could work together to come up with a plan that would satisfy all parties. But you're so busy feeling angry, and sorry for yourself, that—not again,' he warned hardly as March rose angrily to her feet, reaching out to firmly grasp her arms and hold her immobile in front of him. 'You're the most beautiful woman I've ever seen in my life, March,' he breathed raggedly. 'But, without doubt, also the most stupid!'

She opened her mouth to protest, but no words came out. Did Will really think she was the most beautiful woman he had ever seen in his life...?

'Oh, to hell with this.' Will sighed disgustedly. 'This is just one more thing to add to the list of reasons to hate me!' he rasped before his mouth came forcefully down on hers.

It was a kiss of anger, of frustration, of sheer impotence of feeling.

But it was a kiss March responded to…

She loved this man, loved him beyond anyone and anything. And very shortly he was going to walk out of her life and she was never going to see him again.

She sobbed low in her throat, her lips answering the passion between them that it was impossible to deny, Will releasing her arms to pull her against the hardness of his body as he deepened the kiss.

March wound her arms about his waist, pressing close against him, wanting only to be part of him, to forget everything else but Will and the overwhelming love she felt for him.

Which was why she was left totally dazed when Will pulled roughly away from her seconds later to move determinedly to the other side of the bedroom, his expression grimmer than ever. March looked at him questioningly.

'Oh, no you don't.' He gave a self-derisive laugh as he shook his head. 'You may feel you have plenty of reason to hate me, March, but I have no intention of giving you reason to regret me too!'

Her face was pale, her eyes dark. 'But I—'

'Graham and I will be leaving as soon as I've got my few belongings together,' Will cut sharply across the protest she was about to make. 'I doubt we shall see each other again, so—well, goodbye,' he concluded abruptly.

Goodbye.

That had to be the saddest word in the whole of the English language.

Especially when March was saying it to the man she knew she loved above all else…!

She had fallen in love with Will in spite of his connection to Jude Marshall. Despite all her own instincts. Or because of them…

'Will—'

'I think you've already said enough, don't you, March?' he rasped scathingly, blue gaze bleak now that his anger had faded somewhat. 'But Graham is probably more forgiving than me—especially when it comes to the discovery of a new and talented artist,' he added derisively. 'So I'm sure he will be only too happy to talk to you if you should change your mind about his offer of an exhibition.'

Despite his own anger towards her, March knew Will was being more than generous in telling her this. Because he didn't have to, didn't have to do anything more for her. Especially when she had shown him nothing more than ingratitude in return.

She so wanted to cry, so wanted to give in to the terrible pain of Will's departure. But that wouldn't be fair to him, not after all she had already put him through.

Besides, she didn't think she could stand to see his pity if he should realize the reason for her pain…

'Thank you,' she breathed shakily. 'I—have a good journey back to London,' she added lamely.

His mouth twisted ruefully. 'Thanks. About the situation at the agency—'

'I'll—think about it.' She nodded quickly, still not sure what to do about that.

Will grimaced. 'If it comes to light anyway, and anyone finds out that you already knew about it, you could—I'm only saying could—be dragged in as an accomplice. At the very least, be accused of perverting the course of justice by keeping quiet about it,' he warned as she would have protested.

March moistened dry lips. She had already thought of that aspect, knew that she didn't really have any choice but to go to the police with what she had discovered. It just wasn't something she wanted to do.

She nodded. 'I'll—sort it out.'

'Fine.' Will nodded abruptly. 'Take care,' he murmured softly.

He was going. Really going. And there wasn't a thing she could say or do to stop him.

'And you,' she breathed huskily.

He closed the bedroom door quietly behind him as he left, the sound of his feet descending the stairs heard seconds later, followed by the murmur of voices in the kitchen, then the closing of the outer door. And Will was gone.

March wanted to run after him, to tell him how sorry she was for her behaviour, how much she wanted him to stay, how much she— What? Loved him? That really would be unfair. Especially when Will couldn't possibly feel the same way about her.

How could he? When she had been 'rude and obstructive' to him. 'Made his life a misery' almost since the moment he'd arrived.

The tears were falling softly down her cheeks when May entered her bedroom a few minutes later, her sister's expression softening as she saw March's tears.

'Oh, March!' May choked even as she gathered her into her arms.

Oh, March, indeed. What a mess she had made of everything. What an unforgivable mess.

'Are you sure this is the right thing for you to do?'

Will turned briefly from throwing his things into his bag

to look at Graham as he sat on one of the kitchen chairs watching him frowningly. 'The right thing to do would have been never to have come here in the first place,' he bit out harshly, at the same time resuming his haphazard packing.

'You know you don't mean that,' Graham rebuked softly.

'Oh, don't I?' He turned sharply, his anger unmistakable. 'This whole situation has been impossible from the beginning. But only because of March. She's the most impossible woman I have ever met in my life!'

Graham grimaced. 'She's—a little fiery,' he allowed.

'A little!' Will scorned. 'She's rude, sarcastic, outspoken—'

'Beautiful,' Graham put in softly.

'Beauty is as beauty does—or something like that,' Will added impatiently as Graham raised mocking brows. 'Why can't she be like May—still beautiful, but charming and reasonable at the same time?'

Graham held back a smile. 'Because you aren't in love with May.'

Will's eyes widened indignantly at this last statement. 'I'm not in love with March either,' he stated firmly.

'Aren't you?' his friend mused softly.

'No, I am not,' Will assured him firmly. 'Damn it, even having a simple conversation with her turns into a confrontation!'

'But it's worth it, I'm sure,' Graham reasoned teasingly.

Will thought of the occasions he had held March in his arms, of kissing her, caressing her, feeling the silky softness of her skin against his…

'Maybe,' he allowed grudgingly, some of his anger starting to fade.

Besides, who was he most angry with: March for being so unreasonable, or himself for feeling about her the way that he did? Not that he accepted Graham's statement that he was in love with her; how could he possibly be in love with someone he felt like strangling half the time?

Because the other half of the time he just wanted to hold her, to take care of her, to ensure that nothing and no one ever harmed her...!

He was not in love with March Calendar!

'No,' he decided firmly. 'The sooner I'm away from here, the better I will like it.' He turned to slam his bag shut and close the zip. 'I honestly wish I had never met March Calendar!'

'Hello, March,' Graham greeted lightly behind him. 'Anything we can do for you?'

'Very funny, Graham,' Will muttered dryly. 'Aren't you a little old for juvenile tricks like that?' he derided as he turned round.

March stood in the open doorway, her face as white as snow, her eyes so darkly enigmatic it was impossible to tell what colour they were. Or whether or not she had heard his telling statement before Graham had announced her presence!

'Who was being juvenile?' Graham murmured under his breath as he watched the two of them curiously.

If the floor could have opened up and swallowed him, Will knew he would have been for ever thankful. But, of course, it did no such thing, leaving him face to face with March after stating quite categorically that he wished he had never met her!

'March—'

'May wanted you to have this.' March moved to put an envelope down on the kitchen table.

So that she didn't have to actually touch him, Will was sure, his anger returning at this obvious display of her aversion to him. 'What is it?' he snapped.

March shrugged. 'A cheque for the second week's rental on the studio. We don't want it,' she added decisively as Will would have protested. 'You aren't staying here, so we aren't entitled to it,' she told him dismissively.

To say he felt as if he had been slapped on the face for a second time this evening was probably putting it a little strongly, but he certainly felt as if May now supported her sister's stand against him.

'Fine,' he rasped, making no effort to pick up the white envelope.

And he wouldn't pick it up, either, would leave it on the table after he had left. But no doubt the Calendar sisters would find some way of twisting even that gesture round so that he once again came out as the bad guy. He just couldn't seem to win with them.

March turned to Graham, some of her stiffness of manner fading as she gave him a rueful smile. 'I believe I also owe you an apology; I shouldn't have said those things to you earlier.' She grimaced. 'It was just—'

'My friend here getting it wrong, as usual,' Graham accepted, standing up, totally ignoring Will's snort of protest. 'I realize now that my being here at all must have been something of a shock to you,' he sympathized with March. 'I'll give you my card.' He took one from his wallet and held it out to her. 'Think it over and give me a call if you decide to go ahead with the exhibition, after all, hmm?' he encouraged.

Will wasn't in the least fooled by Graham's lightly

encouraging attitude, knew his friend well enough to know that he wasn't about to give up on persuading March into the exhibition, that having 'found' her he wasn't going to let her just disappear again.

On the one hand Will was pleased for March, knew that any exhibition of her work that Graham put on for her was sure to be a success. But on the more negative side, if March went ahead with the exhibition it would mean that she would continue to be in Will's life whether he wanted her to be or not. Graham was an old and valued friend, Will godfather to his youngest daughter, and as such it would be impossible for Graham not to talk about March in the future when the two men met.

But the latter was a selfish attitude, he knew, and one best kept to himself...

'Take the card, March,' he advised dryly.

'If you're sure you don't mind...?' She gave him a searching look.

Will gave a humourless laugh. 'I was the one who brought the two of you together in the first place; why should I mind?'

March shrugged. 'Possibly because you wish you had never met me,' she returned with some of her usual spirit, dark brows raised mockingly.

So she had heard his final statement before Graham had announced her presence! He had thought she must have, but March had just bluntly confirmed it.

Not much he could do about that, was there? Especially as it was true! For numerous reasons...

He gave a rueful shake of his head. 'There's never a hole for you to fall down when you want one!'

March gave the ghost of a smile. 'Join the club,' she returned enigmatically before turning back to Graham. 'Thank you for this.' She indicated the card he had given her. 'I'm not sure yet, but—I will call you and let you know one way or the other.'

'Good enough.' Graham nodded.

'No, it isn't,' Will put in forcefully. 'March, you may never have another opportunity like this one,' he told her impatiently as she looked at him questioningly.

'I'm well aware of that,' she acknowledged huskily. 'But there are—other considerations to take into account, before I come to any decision.'

Will wanted to demand to know what those considerations were, but knew that he had forfeited the right to ask by the fact that he had made that blunt statement about wishing he had never met her, and by March overhearing it. Besides, there was always the possibility that having to see him again might be one of those considerations!

His mouth tightened. 'Just don't leave Graham waiting too long, March,' he bit out tersely.

She gave him a dismissive look before turning back to Graham. 'I really am grateful for your interest,' she assured him with much more warmth than she had just shown Will.

And could he really blame her for that, after what she had overheard?

But there was no way he could retract what he had said without making the situation worse than it already was. If that were possible!

He really needed to get away from here, away from March, to sit calmly and collectedly and work out exactly what it was he felt for her. Because he had just realized that leaving her was probably the hardest thing he had ever done in his life!

But leave her he must. For both their sakes.

But March was the one leaving now, raising a hand in farewell before quietly closing the door behind her.

'If I weren't already a married man…' Graham murmured appreciatively.

'But you are,' Will reminded sharply, a shaft of—something, something painful, shooting through him at the other man's obvious admiration of March. 'And likely to remain that way,' he added with satisfaction.

Graham gave an acknowledging inclination of his head. 'But you aren't,' he returned dryly. 'And I would say it's very unlikely that you will remain that way,' he added teasingly.

Will gave a dismissive shake of his head. 'Let's just go, hmm, Graham.' He picked up his bag and briefcase. 'The sooner I'm out of here, the better I'll like it.'

His friend chuckled softly as he joined him by the door. 'You can run but you can't hide,' he rejoined enigmatically.

Will gave him a narrow-eyed glare, not fooled for a moment. 'I'm not even going to qualify that remark with an answer. Just move it,' he grated hardly.

Graham was still chuckling as he clattered down the metal stairs ahead of him.

Whereas Will couldn't see anything funny about this situation, lingering to take one last glance over at the farmhouse before getting into his car.

The light was still on in the kitchen, and Will could easily imagine the two sisters, sitting at the kitchen table, drinking tea or coffee, talking softly together.

Would March do anything about Clive Carter?

Would the sisters sell the farm?

Would May take the film role if it were offered?

Would March take up Graham's offer of an exhibition of her work?

In only a matter of days he had become completely embroiled in the life of the Calendar sisters. And with his abrupt departure he was giving up the right to an answer to any of those questions...

CHAPTER FOURTEEN

'HE HASN'T gone, you know, March.'

March looked up from where she had been pushing the food around on her plate in an effort to look as if she were really eating her dinner, when in actual fact she hadn't been able to eat anything for days. Her throat felt dry all the time from the tears she cried whenever she was alone, and the thought of actually having to swallow anything other than the strong cups of tea or coffee she was constantly making was complete anathema to her.

'March,' May pushed strongly. 'I said—'

'I heard what you said,' March assured her wearily. 'I just didn't understand it,' she admitted ruefully.

May sighed, her frown one of concern rather than censure. 'You really can't go on like this, you know, March. You aren't eating, you aren't sleeping—oh, I've heard you pacing around in your bedroom at night,' she said firmly. 'You've lost weight the last three days, March, and it really doesn't suit you.'

'Thanks!' She smiled ruefully.

May shrugged. 'It's the truth, and you know it. And what I said just now was that Will hasn't gone.'

March frowned uncomprehendingly. 'Gone where?'

'Don't play with your food,' her sister reproved lightly, standing up to move the untouched plate of food from in front of March. 'Uncle Sid saw Will's car over at the Hanworth Estate earlier today; I've been debating all day whether or not I should tell you,' she admitted with a grimace. 'But looking at you this evening—this can't go on, you know, March.' She gave a determined shake of her head.

March sat stunned by the fact that Will was still in the area. On Monday evening he had said—what had he said, exactly? That he had to get away from here, from the farm, from her, not that he was actually going back to London. She was the one who had assumed that.

She swallowed hard, her throat dry. 'So he's still around.' She shrugged. 'What does that have to do with me?'

May frowned. 'March, you're in love with the man—'

'I am not! Well...okay, maybe I am,' she acknowledged gruffly at her sister's reproving look. What was the point of denying it? She had all the symptoms of unrequited love!

'Well?' May prompted impatiently when March added nothing to her original statement.

'Well what?' She stood up, moving restlessly around the kitchen. 'He certainly doesn't feel the same way about me!' To her dismay her voice broke emotionally.

The last three days since Will's abrupt departure had been awful. She was in love with a man who—

'You didn't hear him on Monday evening, May,' she cried painfully. 'He told Graham Whitford that he wished he had never met me!' She buried her face in her hands, the tears starting to fall once again.

May's arms came around March as she patted her back soothingly. 'I'm sure that he does, too,' she acknowledged dryly.

March raised her head sharply. 'Well, then?' she snapped defensively.

'Oh, March.' Her sister shook her head, frustrated affection on her face as she held March at arm's length.

'Of course Will wishes he had never met you—goodness knows you aren't the easiest person in the world to love! Oh, I don't have a problem with it,' she assured hastily at March's woebegone look. 'But I'm your sister. Will hasn't known whether he's on his head or his heels since the moment he met you!'

'Rubbish,' she dismissed hardly, moving away from May to stare sightlessly out of the window.

She loved this place, loved her sisters, and until a few days ago she had been perfectly happy with her life. Now it all felt something like a prison, holding her captive here, with no reprieve in sight.

'After I spoke to Uncle Sid this morning I checked around in town for the likeliest hotel for Will to be staying—'

'You didn't?' March gasped, her eyes wide as she turned to face May.

'Oh, don't worry.' May smiled ruefully. 'I haven't spoken to him or anything like that. I just wanted to know if he had returned to the same hotel. He has,' she added with satisfaction.

'But why did you go to that trouble?' March shook her head dazedly.

'So that I could tell you, of course,' her sister returned in patiently.

'But—'

'March, if you don't go and see Will then I'm afraid I will have to. And I think it might be better if it were you,' May added huskily.

'And just what would I say to him?' she cried frustratedly.

'Well, an apology might not be a bad way to start—'

'I did that on Monday evening—'

'As I understand it, you apologized to Graham

Whitford on Monday evening,' May cut in determinedly. 'Who, incidentally, isn't going to wait for ever for you to call him and accept his offer,' she added frowningly.

'But I—'

'You are going to accept, March,' May told her firmly. 'It's what you've always wanted.' Her voice softened affectionately. 'And you aren't going to let pride stand in your way of accepting. But first you have to apologize to Will, and thank him for going to the trouble of giving you this opportunity.'

She knew that, had known it for the last three days. It was not knowing where Will was, or how to contact him, that had made this time seem so much bleaker.

'What if he won't see me?' She frowned her uncertainty.

May gave a chuckle. 'He'll see you. But if you want an excuse for turning up at his hotel room...' she moved to pick up the envelope that sat on one of the worktops '...he didn't take this cheque with him when he left.' She handed it to March.

He probably wouldn't take it now, either, and it was a pretty feeble excuse for going to see him in the first place. But it was better than nothing...

'Okay.' She took the envelope, turning to leave.

'March, aren't you going to change or—or at least smarten up your appearance before you go?' May frowned concernedly.

She was looking less than her best, March knew, wearing no make-up, had lived in jeans and jumpers the last three days, and her hair could probably do with a wash too. But if she took the time to smarten herself up, as May put it, she might just lose her nerve and not go at all.

'Never mind,' May added hastily, obviously having

read the same thing from March's expression. 'I don't suppose Will will be too interested in the way you look, anyway—I didn't mean it like that, March.' She chuckled ruefully at March's pained grimace. 'If I'm right about the way Will feels about you, then he isn't going to care what you look like, he'll just be glad to see you.'

March had no idea how Will felt about her, only knew that she had to see him, whether he wanted to see her or not.

Although she didn't feel quite so sure about that an hour later when Will opened the door to his hotel suite, his look of polite enquiry turning to a scowl as he saw it was her standing there!

March was the last person he had expected to see this evening. The last person he had ever expected to see at all!

In fact, he was so surprised to see her that it didn't even cross his mind how she had known he was here…!

His gaze ate her up hungrily, noting the dark shadows beneath her eyes, the gaunt paleness of her face—she had never looked more beautiful to him!

'March,' he greeted huskily—inanely—wondering why it was that whenever he was around this woman he ceased to be a confidently articulate man and became a dumbstruck idiot.

She still didn't speak, her eyes—those beautiful grey-green eyes—filling with tears as she looked up at him.

'What is it?' His voice sharpened in concern at her continued silence, a dark frown on his brow. 'Is it May? January or Max?'

She smiled through her tears. 'No. But thank you for your concern,' she added throatily.

Will frowned his confusion. 'Then what—is it Carter?' He scowled. 'Did he turn nasty, after all?'

'No, it isn't Clive, either.' She gave a rueful shake of her head. 'Actually, you're totally wrong about that situation. You see—'

'Come inside and talk,' Will cut in briskly, not at all happy talking to her in a hotel corridor like this, where anyone might stroll along and overhear them.

She hesitated. 'If you're sure I'm not interrupting…?'

His mouth twisted ruefully. 'I'm sure you'll be pleased to know that the only thing you're interrupting is the final adjustments on my plans for the health and country club!' Although, as he saw her frown deepen, he wasn't sure that was an altogether diplomatic subject for him to have mentioned!

But to his relief March merely nodded before accompanying him inside his hotel suite.

She gave him a hesitant, totally un-March smile, deepening his concern that something was seriously wrong.

'You were saying…?' he prompted frowningly.

'Oh, yes.' She nodded, seeming relieved to have a neutral subject she could talk about. 'I'm afraid you totally misunderstood the situation at the estate agency; Michelle was the one who was buying properties under value and then selling them on.'

'Michelle…?' Will couldn't hide his disbelief; to him Michelle Jones most resembled a timid little mouse, didn't seem at all the type to become involved in such subterfuge.

'Yes,' March sighed. 'Apparently she thought Clive was tiring of her, and the estate agency, decided that she needed a little nest egg of her own for that eventuality.' March shrugged ruefully.

Will was stunned. Absolutely stunned. 'You've spoken to her?'

'Oh, yes.' March sighed again. 'She came to see me at the farm yesterday. Apparently she and Clive have discussed the whole thing. Michelle is going to go to the police and tell them exactly what she has done. But first she and Clive are going to be married.'

'She may go to prison for what she's done.' Will frowned.

March grimaced. 'They know that. He has a strange way of showing it, but it seems that Clive loves her and is going to stand by her. I— Would you mind if I sat down? I—I'm really not feeling so good.' She sat down abruptly.

She didn't look so good either, Will realized as he frowned his concern. Her jeans hung loosely on her, those dark shadows beneath her eyes and the gauntness of her face taking on another aspect entirely.

He moved to the mini-bar, taking out a small bottle of whisky and pouring it into one of the glasses before handing it to March. 'Drink it,' he advised gruffly.

She looked up to give him a smile. 'As long as you don't complain when it makes me drunk; I'm afraid I haven't eaten very much the last few days.'

Neither had Will, if the truth were known. He simply didn't have any appetite. And as for sleeping...! Come to think of it, he probably looked as ill as March said she felt!

'The last three days, in fact,' March added huskily.

Three days. Precisely the amount of time that had passed since the last time the two of them had spoken...

'Drink it,' he repeated softly, going down on his haunches beside her chair to look at her concernedly.

'March, what are you doing here?' he prompted gently, at the same time taking one of her hands in his.

Even her fingers were slimmer, just skin covering the delicate bones beneath, a slight tremor to that delicacy as his thumb lightly caressed the back of her hand.

She took a large gulp of the whisky before answering him, the fiery liquid bringing a little colour to the paleness of her cheeks. 'I didn't realize you were still in the area until Uncle Sid saw you earlier today—May was the one who found out you were back at this hotel—Will, I owe you an apology.' Her voice was huskier still from the effects of the whisky. 'I realize you were just trying to be helpful. By sending some of my paintings to Graham,' she explained abruptly. 'I—I've decided to accept his offer.' She looked at him searchingly, as if unsure of what his response was going to be to this decision.

'I'm glad,' Will assured her unhesitantly. 'Really glad,' he added with satisfaction. 'You're good, March. Very good.'

She gave a rueful smile. 'Well, I don't know about that. But Graham seems to think I might be too, so let's hope you're both right.'

'We are,' he told her with certainty. 'Was that—is the apology the only reason you came here?' he prompted carefully.

March gave a self-derisive smile. 'Isn't that enough?'

He grimaced. Not nearly enough, as far as he was concerned.

The last three days had been purgatory for him, with March so close and yet emotionally so far away, and yet he had been loath to leave the area. He hadn't slept much, and food had held no interest for him; the only thing left for him to do had been to concentrate on fin-

ishing Jude's plans for the health and country club. And
even that irritated him, with its indisputable connection
to March and the farm she had lived in all her life.

But now, after those awful three days, March was here
with him, and the thought of letting her just get up and
walk out the door was completely unacceptable to him.

He straightened abruptly. 'In that case, I have something that needs to be said,' he bit out grimly, thrusting
his hands into his denim pockets; if he didn't he might
just reach down and pull her into his arms, kiss her until
she was senseless, and to hell with any explanations!

March looked up at him warily. 'Yes?'

Will looked down at her frustratedly, wondering
where to begin, what to say. And then knowing there
was only one thing he really wanted to say. Only one
thing that mattered.

He drew in a ragged breath. 'March, will you marry
me?'

There.

He had said it.

Said the one thing that had been uppermost in his
mind for the last three days without her in his life.

Now it only remained for March to give him another
slap in the face, either verbally or physically!

CHAPTER FIFTEEN

PERHAPS she was drunk, after all, because Will couldn't really have just asked her to marry him. Could he…?

She stared up at him disbelievingly, unable to read anything from his guarded expression. Except…

Now that she looked at him more closely, Will didn't look a lot better than she did, dark shadows beneath those gloriously blue eyes, his face thinner too, an unhealthy pallor to the gauntness of his cheeks.

Perhaps he had been as miserable as she had the last three days?

Perhaps for the same reason—because he was also in love with her!

She moistened dry lips before carefully placing the empty whisky glass down on the coffee-table in front of her, standing up to move only inches away from him as she looked up unflinchingly into his face.

His guarded look flickered and died, to be replaced by—by what? Uncertainty? Wariness? Hope?

It was all three of those, giving March the confidence to reach up and gently caress one hard cheek before standing on tiptoe and kissing him gently on the lips.

Will groaned low in his throat, his arms moving to gather her close against him as he deepened the kiss, parting her lips beneath his as he drank in her fullness.

March needed no further encouragement, her arms moving about his shoulders as she pressed close against him, her hands tangled in the blond silkiness of the hair at his nape, wanting this kiss to just go on and on.

But it didn't, of course, Will raising his head with obvious reluctance as he looked down at her quizzically. 'I hope that was a yes to my marriage proposal...?'

He still sounded so unsure, so unlike his usual confident self, that March could only gaze up at him.

'This is not the time for one of your uncharacteristic silences, March,' he told her frustratedly, his hands firm on her upper arms as he shook her slightly. 'I love you. The last three days without you have shown me only too clearly that I don't want to live my life without you in it—'

'Even though I'm rude, and prickly, and outspoken, and far too quick to jump to conclusions—'

'All that!' he confirmed laughingly. 'You're March,' he added simply. 'Every delectable, contrary, stubborn inch of you—and I love every part of you!' he assured her huskily, his gaze intent on the beauty of her face.

'Oh, Will,' she choked emotionally, her hands tightening on the broadness of his shoulders. 'I love you too. I love you so much! This last three days have been—'

'Forget them,' he cut in decisively. 'If you say yes to my marriage proposal we will never be apart again!' His eyes glowed deeply blue as he looked down at her.

March looked up at him, no longer bothering to hide the way she felt about him, the love she felt for him shining in her grey-green eyes. 'Yes,' she breathed forcefully. 'Oh, yes...!'

Will swept her back into his arms, his kiss so poignantly beautiful that March found herself crying once again.

'Hey,' he raised his head to chide gently. 'You aren't supposed to cry at a time like this,' he teased.

She wiped the tears away with the back of her hand. 'I seem to have done nothing *but* cry the last three days.

I thought you had gone, that I would never see you again, that I—'

'It's over, March,' Will assured her firmly. 'I love you—'

'And I love you,' she told him fervently.

'Then that's all that matters,' he told her before he bent his head and kissed her once again, his hands lightly cradling each side of her face as he looked into her eyes. 'My parents are going to love you,' he said with certainty.

His parents...!

She hadn't given Will's family a thought, been consumed by the fact that Will loved her as she loved him.

She still found that hard to believe, knew that she hadn't exactly been very welcoming when he'd first arrived, even less so since she had discovered his connection to Jude Marshall.

Jude Marshall...!

What on earth was he going to think? First his lawyer had defected and intended marrying one of the Calendar sisters, and now his architect was about to do the same thing. The man was going to think it was some sort of Machiavellian plot against him by the Calendar sisters.

'I doubt your current employer is going to be too pleased.' March grimaced, very much aware that Jude Marshall was Will's friend as much as anything else.

Will shrugged. 'We'll talk about Jude in a few minutes. I haven't kissed you nearly enough yet to be able to talk about such inanities.' He pulled her down into a chair with him, settling March comfortably on his knees before kissing her once again.

Heaven.

Sheer heaven.

And she was going to be with Will for the rest of her

life. Nothing, and no one, meant more to her than he did.

They never would.

It was a long time later, Will having ordered dinner to be served to them in his hotel suite, that he returned to those 'inanities'.

'Eat, March,' he encouraged, touching her hand lightly as she looked at him rather than eating any of the melon and strawberries on the plate in front of her. 'If just now was anything to go by, we're both going to need to build up our strength for our honeymoon!' he added teasingly, rewarded by the becoming blush that highlighted her cheeks. 'You are adorable, do you know that?' He chuckled delightedly.

She shook her head. 'I still can't believe all of this is true. I was so miserable earlier when I thought you had completely gone from our lives.' She gave a shudder of remembered pain.

Will's hand tightened on hers. 'With your agreement, I would like our engagement to be a short one?'

'As short as you like,' she said instantly. 'Although I would obviously like my sisters to be present. But as Max and January will be back at the weekend...'

He couldn't wait to see the look on Max's face when he was told of Will's engagement to March!

'And May?' he prompted frowningly.

March frowned slightly. 'She says she isn't going to accept the part in the film. I have no idea why,' she added as Will was about to ask. 'She just came back from her weekend away and stated quite categorically that she wasn't going to do it. Which brings us back to the same problem concerning whether or not to sell the farm,' she realized frowningly.

'Hmm.' Will got up from the table, moving to pick up the two envelopes that sat on the desk in front of the window. 'I've drawn up two plans here.' He held up the envelopes. 'One includes your farm. The other one doesn't. Which do you think I should submit to Jude?'

March grimaced as she looked at the two envelopes. 'Perhaps we should let May choose?' she said finally.

'Perhaps we should,' he agreed slowly, putting the envelopes down, knowing there was something else they needed to discuss. 'March, I live in London most of the time—'

'I know that,' she cut in reassuringly. 'May was the one who found out you were still here, and told me about it,' she said softly. 'I'm sure she is well aware that if— if the two of us ever got together that I would move to London to live with you.'

'But if January and Max are moving to London too… May can't run the farm on her own.' Will frowned. He liked May, liked her a lot, was looking forward to having her as his 'sister'.

'Who knows, my exhibition may be a wonderful success,' March told him brightly, 'and then I can still help May out financially if in no other way. Will, I'm sure we'll be able to work something out,' she said determinedly. 'After all,' she added mischievously, 'if you and I have found a happy ending, I'm sure there must be one for May too. After all, having brought the two of us up, she deserves it so much more than January or I do!'

'I'm very fond of May, and I'm sure she deserves to be happy.' Will reached down and pulled March to her feet. 'But no more than you do. And I intend to make sure that in future you are very happy, March Calendar, soon-to-be-Davenport,' he promised huskily.

'I'm already happier than I ever dreamed possible,' she assured him with a glowing smile, standing on tiptoe and kissing him with all the love she had previously kept hidden behind her prickly exterior.

Heaven.

Sheer heaven.

And he was going to spend the rest of his life with March. Nothing, and no one, meant more to him than she did.

They never would.

The world's bestselling romance series.

HARLEQUIN®
Presents

Seduction and Passion Guaranteed!

Mama Mia!

ITALIAN HUSBANDS

They're tall, dark...and ready to marry!

Don't delay, pick up the next story in
this great new miniseries...pronto!

On sale this month
MARCO'S PRIDE by Jane Porter #2385

Coming in April
HIS INHERITED BRIDE by Jacqueline Baird #2385

Don't miss
May 2004
THE SICILIAN HUSBAND by Kate Walker #2393

July 2004
THE ITALIAN'S DEMAND by Sara Wood #2405

Pick up a Harlequin Presents® novel and you will
enter a world of spine-tingling passion and
provocative, tantalizing romance!

Available wherever Harlequin books are sold.

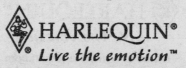

HARLEQUIN®
Live the emotion™

Visit us at www.eHarlequin.com

The world's bestselling romance series.

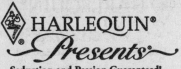

HARLEQUIN®
Presents

Seduction and Passion Guaranteed!

We are pleased to announce
Sandra Marton's fantastic new series

The
O'CONNELLS

In order to marry, they've got to gamble on love!

Don't miss...

KEIR O'CONNELL'S MISTRESS

Keir O'Connell knew it was time to leave Las Vegas when he became consumed with desire for a dancer. The heat of the desert must have addled his brain! He headed east and set himself up in business—but thoughts of the dancing girl wouldn't leave his head.
And then one day there she was, Cassie...

Harlequin Presents #2309
On sale March 2003

Pick up a Harlequin Presents® novel and you will enter a world of spine-tingling passion and provocative, tantalizing romance!

Available wherever Harlequin books are sold.

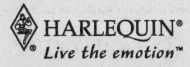

HARLEQUIN®
Live the emotion™

Visit us at www.eHarlequin.com

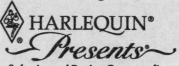

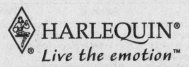

The world's bestselling romance series.

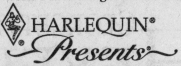

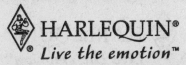